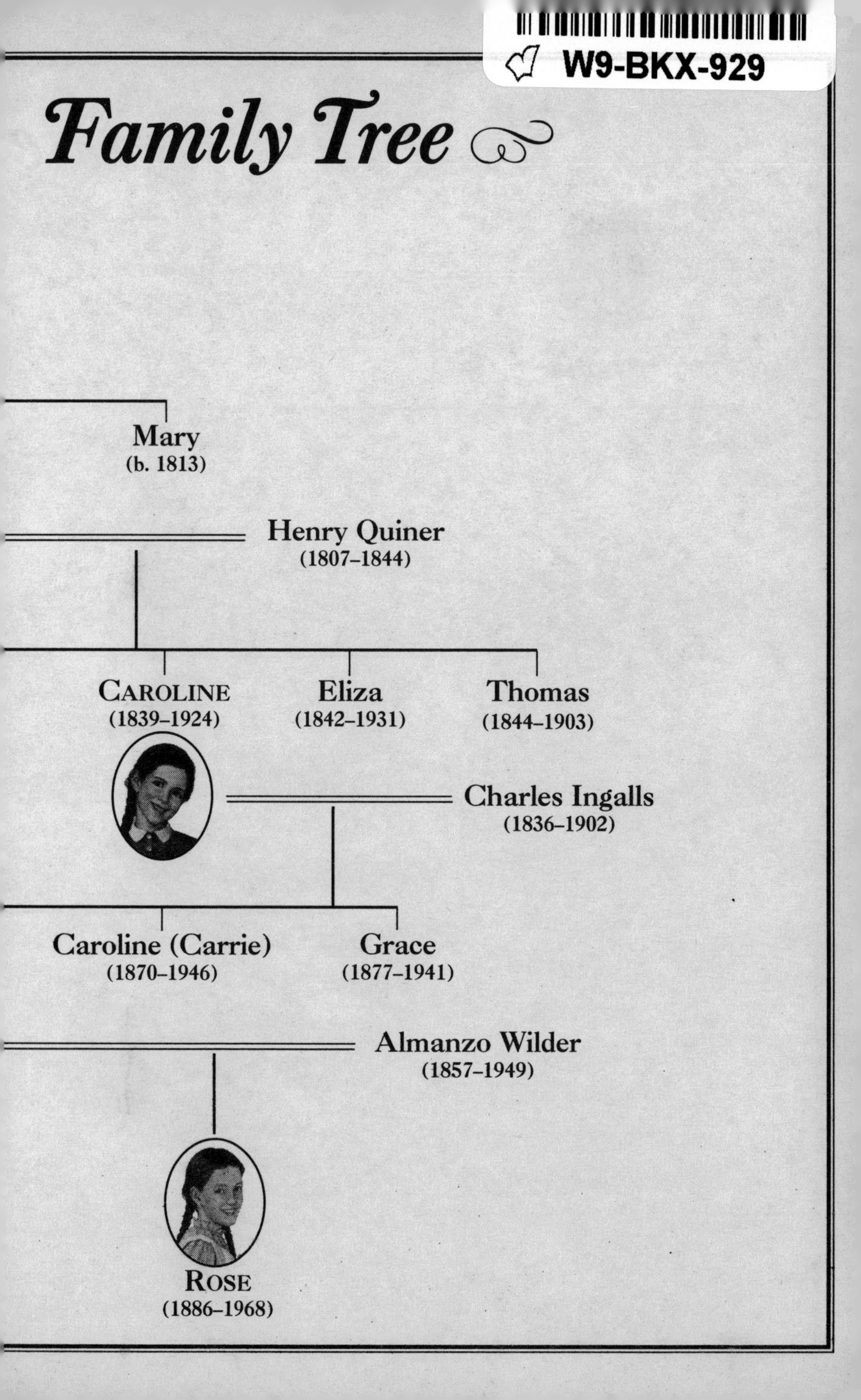

W9-BKX-929
Family Tree
Mary
(b. 1813)
Henry Quiner
(1807–1844)
Caroline
(1839–1924)
Eliza
(1842–1931)
Thomas
(1844–1903)
Charles Ingalls
(1836–1902)
Caroline (Carrie)
(1870–1946)
Grace
(1877–1941)
Almanzo Wilder
(1857–1949)
Rose
(1886–1968)

Little City *by the* Lake

STUTSMAN COUNTY LIBRARY
910 5TH ST S E
JAMESTOWN, N D 58401
WITHDRAWN

Celia Wilkins

Illustrations by Dan Andreasen

HarperTrophy®
An Imprint of HarperCollins*Publishers*

The author wishes to thank Abigail Theys, as well as the staff from the Milwaukee County Historical Society for assistance in researching pioneer life in Milwaukee. For additional research into customs, dress, and general history of the period, many thanks to Amy Edgar Sklansky and William F. Jannke, III.

HarperCollins, Harper Trophy®, ®, Little House®, and The Caroline Years™
are trademarks of HarperCollins Publishers Inc.

Little City by the Lake
Text copyright © 2003 by HarperCollins Publishers Inc.
Illustrations © 2003 by Dan Andreasen
All rights reserved. No part of this book may be used or reproduced in any manner whatsoever without written permission except in the case of brief quotations embodied in critical articles and reviews.
Printed in the United States of America. For information address HarperCollins Children's Books, a division of HarperCollins Publishers, 1350 Avenue of the Americas, New York, NY 10019.
www.littlehousebooks.com

Library of Congress Cataloging-in-Publication Data
Wilkins, Celia.
Little city by the lake / Celia Wilkins ; illustrations by Dan Andreasen.
p. cm.
Summary: Fifteen-year-old Caroline Quiner, who will become the mother of Laura Ingalls Wilder, moves to Milwaukee in 1855 to experience city life and attend school.
ISBN 0-06-027006-3 — ISBN 0-06-440735-7 (pbk.)
1. Ingalls, Caroline Lake Quiner—Juvenile fiction. [1. Ingalls, Caroline Lake Quiner—Fiction. 2. Wilder, Laura Ingalls, 1867–1957—Family—Fiction. 3. Schools—Fiction. 4. Milwaukee (Wis.)—History—19th century—Fiction.] I. Title. II. Series: Little House. III. Andreasen, Dan, ill.
PZ7.W648498 Li 2003 2002014920
[Fic]—dc21 CIP
AC

1 2 3 4 5 6 7 8 9 10
❖
First Harper Trophy edition, 2003

Author's Note

Many years before she ever put pen to paper to create what would become the Little House books, Laura Ingalls Wilder wrote to her aunt Martha Quiner Carpenter, and asked her to "tell the story of those days" when she and Laura's mother, Caroline, were young girls. Laura's mother had never talked much about her childhood in the newly settled Wisconsin territory, and so Aunt Martha wrote several letters to Laura filled with memories of the Quiners' day-to-day life during the 1840s and 1850s. These letters became the basis for the Caroline series.

In Little City by the Lake, *I have sought to present the most realistic portrait possible of Caroline Quiner's life as a girl and young woman, while striving to stay true to Laura's own depiction of her beloved Ma in the Little House books.*

—C.W.

Contents

Milwaukee!

"Milwaukee! Great city of Milwaukee! Next and final stop!"

Caroline heard the driver's sharp call above the clattering of the wheels and the thrumming of the horses' hooves. She had only a moment to feel a tingle of nervous excitement before the stagecoach lurched suddenly to the left. For what seemed like the hundredth time that morning, she was thrown against the hard wall of the coach.

"So sorry, my dear," the lady beside her whispered, digging a sharp elbow into

Caroline's side as she pulled herself upright and straightened her bonnet and skirt.

Caroline wanted to give a polite reply, but she was too winded to speak. When Pa had taken her to meet the stagecoach last night in Concord, she had been shocked at how crowded it was. Inside the coach, the hard wooden benches were packed with bodies. She had only been able to squeeze in at the very end of a long row. At first she thought herself lucky to be sitting near the wall, but soon she had discovered how uncomfortable it was.

All night long, the stagecoach bumped and jolted over the rough dirt road. Each time it veered to the left, Caroline was pushed hard against the wall, the weight of all the other passengers pressing against her. During the day, the dust streaming through the open window next to her had been almost unbearable.

"Keep your kerchief over your mouth!" the lady next to her had advised right away, and Caroline had done as she suggested. But even so, her mouth and throat were so dry from the dust, it felt like she had swallowed a bucketful of ashes.

"I do so wish we could take you to Milwaukee ourselves," Mother had fretted several times before Caroline left. "I am not convinced it is a proper way for you to travel."

"Oh, Mother, it is 1855!" Martha had exclaimed. Martha had become very opinionated since she had turned eighteen. "Plenty of ladies ride the stagecoach these days. And remember how Miss May came to us by coach, and that was four years ago!"

"I will be fine," Caroline had spoken up, not because she had wanted to ride the stagecoach by herself, but because she had not wanted to worry Mother. September was one of the busiest months on the little farm. She knew Pa could not spare the time or the wagon to take her himself.

"Well, your uncle will be there to meet you." Mother had sighed and Caroline had nodded and tried to look brave. Looking brave was something she had been doing for months, ever since Uncle Elisha's letter had arrived.

In his letter, Uncle Elisha had told them of a

college for young ladies that had recently opened in Milwaukee. He wondered if Mother would want to send Caroline to attend it.

"Now that our boys are grown and our dear Mother Quiner is no longer with us, we have ample space in our home," Uncle Elisha had written. "It would please us immensely to have Caroline stay with us for the school year while she furthers her education in our fair city. Mother Quiner often spoke of Caroline's desire to become a schoolteacher. And this would be the perfect opportunity."

Mother had read the letter out loud at supper one night, and Caroline had felt many emotions at once: grief over her beloved grandmother's passing the year before, and excitement at the thought of attending a college. She had also felt fear.

"It *is* a wonderful opportunity, Caroline," Mother had said. "You will be sixteen soon, and you will be able to study to become a teacher at a real college."

Caroline was different from her sisters, Martha and Eliza. She loved school, and she wanted more than anything to be a teacher. She knew she was one of the best scholars in Concord, but how could she possibly compare with scholars in a big city? And how could she leave her friends and her home and her family?

"How can we afford it?" Caroline had found herself blurting out—one of the many questions swirling around inside her head.

"Now, Caroline, you let your mother and me worry about that." Pa had spoken up in his quiet, measured way. Pa had been Mr. Holbrook until he married Mother five years ago.

"It will be just like when I was a girl attending seminary back in Boston," Mother had said brightly, settling the matter for good. "I am so glad you will be able to have this experience, Caroline. It will last you a lifetime."

Now it seemed to Caroline that riding in the stagecoach would last a lifetime. All told, it was a very unpleasant way to travel. The ride was very rough, and the passengers were cross due to the cramped conditions. Only the two men sitting directly across the tiny aisle from

Caroline, their knees almost touching hers, seemed to be having a fine time.

"Whoa, Nelly!" they shouted each time the stagecoach bumped into the air. One man was quite large, with a round red face, and the other was skinny, with big yellow teeth.

"This driver will get us there quick enough," the large man said, taking something out of his coat pocket and offering it to his friend.

"If he don't kill us first!" the skinny man said, guffawing loudly.

A sharp, sweet smell filled the air, and Caroline realized with dismay that the two men must be passing liquor back and forth between them in a silver flask. She tried to ignore the men, but it was difficult since she sat facing them.

"Can't wait to get back home," the large man said. "I have been all over this wondrous state—and to a few others besides."

"And you still fancy Milwaukee, do ye?" his companion asked.

"I do, my friend. I do. And mark my words,

Milwaukee is a little city now, but one day it will be a great city in our young nation. Everybody brags on Chicago, but for my money, I'd crown Milwaukee Queen of the Lake."

There was a pause as the flask went back and forth again, and then the large man leaned forward in his seat. "Ever been there, little lady?"

Caroline realized with a start that the man was looking right at her. She did not want to answer. Mother had told her not to speak to strangers. But she could not ignore a question either when the stranger was staring her right in the face.

"No, sir," she managed to say.

"What's a pretty country girl like you doing going to the big city?" the man asked, grinning at her.

Caroline felt her cheeks growing hot. She glanced around. Now everyone in the stagecoach was looking at her.

"I will be going to school," she said, trying to sound grown-up. "I am studying to be a teacher."

"Pshaw," the man said. "You're too pretty to be an old-maid schoolteacher."

Caroline looked down at the leather satchel Pa had lent her. She was clutching the handle so tightly, her knuckles were white. She did not know what to do or say.

"You two keep your thoughts to yourselves and stop badgering this poor girl," the lady beside her scolded.

"Just making small talk to pass the time, ma'am," the big man said, winking at Caroline. "No harm meant, missy."

Caroline kept her eyes on her lap for some time, not daring to look up at the men. After a while, someone in the coach said, "Ah, the plank road at last! We'll have a smoother ride now."

Right away the sound of the horses' hooves became an even clip-clop and the ride did indeed become smoother. The dust cleared a little. Caroline could finally see something of the countryside they were traveling through.

The land was marshy, with stalks of wild rice and bunches of tall, yellowing grasses blowing in the breeze. Thickets of tamarack and cedar lined the road, along with plum trees and patches of wild rosebushes.

After a while the marshland turned to smooth fields that surged up into high grassy bluffs and fell back into cleared farmland with houses and barns and fences. The road itself became crowded with wagons and carts and livestock, and the stagecoach was forced to slow down.

A group of small children dashed out of a barn and went running alongside the road, yelling up at the stagecoach. Caroline had a sudden memory of seeing the stagecoach for the first time long ago in Brookfield. How fast and frightening it had been as it dashed through the streets! How elegant all the people had appeared riding inside! Now here she was, so many years later, riding in a stagecoach herself.

Soon the simple farmhouses began to give way to buildings made of brick. The brick was a lovely cream color that seemed to glow in the morning light. Once more the land rose upward, and Caroline glimpsed several grand houses built high atop the grassy bluffs.

"Ah!" The big man let out a great sigh. "Milwaukee at last."

The stagecoach made a sharp turn and they were trotting down a wide street lined on both sides with the tallest buildings Caroline had ever seen. The buildings stood three and four stories high, and they were all made of the same cream-colored brick. Many had colorful signs and awnings running along the fronts. Caroline tried to read as many of the signs as she could:

Fogerty's Dry Goods—
Best Selection Anywhere!
Smithson's Gun Shop
McCurdy Silversmithing
Ralston Bakers
Milliner—Ladies' Hats for Sale

Crowds of people, mostly men, were walking in the street or on the plank sidewalks that ran in front of the buildings. The stagecoach made another quick turn, and they traveled over a wide, flat bridge made of planks. Water shimmered on both sides of the coach.

Buildings came right up to the water's edge.

"The Milwaukee River," the large man commented. "Cuts the city in half."

After they had crossed the river, the sky was lost, and they were driving in shadow between very tall buildings on both sides. The streets were teeming with people and horsemen and carriages and carts. There were even a few pigs and dogs running about.

"Clear the way! Clear the way!" the stagecoach driver yelled in his gruff voice.

Pigs squealed and dogs barked. Surprised and irritated faces flashed by, and Caroline heard a few curses being hurled back at the driver. She remembered how Mother had told her that in many ways Milwaukee was still a rough frontier town, and that she must always be on her guard.

"Whoa!" the driver yelled, and at last the stagecoach jerked to a halt. It took all of Caroline's strength not to pitch forward into the laps of the men across from her.

"Praise the lord," the lady next to her said under her breath. She gave Caroline a tired smile and then began patting her face with a new handkerchief she pulled from her purse. Caroline couldn't help but notice that the lady's handkerchief came away dull with dust.

"Oh no!" she thought, touching her own face with her gloved fingertips. She must look as grimy as she felt. And she would be seeing Uncle Elisha and Aunt Jane for the first time in many years. She wondered if they would recognize her and what they would think of her.

Frantically, Caroline pulled out a clean handkerchief from her satchel and patted her cheeks. She looked down at her dress. At least it did not look crumpled. The blue serge Mother had chosen was pretty, but it was practical too. The skirt flared out beautifully and was edged with a bold geometric trim of black velvet. Mother had made a matching casaque jacket with lovely peg-top sleeves. And Caroline had trimmed her new straw bonnet with dark blue ribbon. The whole outfit had been copied straight out of *Godey's Lady's Book*, and Caroline felt very grown-up wearing it.

"Good luck with your schooling," the lady beside her said.

"Thank you, ma'am," Caroline replied politely, and then the doors on both sides of the stagecoach were thrown open.

"Ladies first! Make way for the ladies!"

The call was made but ignored, as all the passengers scrambled to descend. A hand was held out to Caroline, and she was swept to the ground. She took a few steps and then stopped and stood uncertainly. It still felt like she was riding on the stagecoach. Her knees were wobbly and her stomach was queasy. It did not help that the air was hot and thick. Caroline closed her eyes to steady herself. When she opened them, a small boy with a very dirty face was staring up at her.

"Carry yer bag, miss?" he asked.

Caroline shook her head and looked around for Uncle Elisha, but she saw only strangers. Men rushed by, pushing carts or carrying heavy burlap sacks. It was so noisy, Caroline felt like covering her ears—and her nose too. The air was ripe with a strong smell of manure and of fish. Caroline realized they must be near the place where the boats docked. Piles of lumber were stacked up beside plank warehouses and rows of barrels and crates. Looking between the buildings, Caroline caught sight of tall white sails and a sparkle of water.

"Calhoun Hotel—best place in town. Clean beds. Good food. Just right for a lady."

Caroline realized that the boy was still there, and he was still talking to her.

"Which bag is yourn?" he asked, tugging on her skirt.

Caroline turned and pointed to her trunk being lifted from the top of the stagecoach. In an instant, the boy had rushed forward to grab the trunk. He did not look big enough to carry it, but with a mighty heave he began dragging it across the cobblestones.

"My uncle is coming for me," Caroline called, but the boy was already far ahead of her.

"Don't you fret none, miss," he yelled over his shoulder. "I'll take care of you good and proper!"

"Wait, wait!" Caroline cried, stumbling

forward through the crowd. She felt tears welling up in her eyes. She was trying to keep sight of the boy and the trunk, when suddenly she heard a deep voice say, "There she is!" and she was looking up into a familiar face. Her heart leaped inside her chest. For a moment she thought she was looking into the face of her father, but she knew that was impossible. Her father had died long ago, when she was only five years old.

"Are you too grown-up to hug your uncle?" the deep voice asked teasingly. Brown eyes crinkled at the corners, and the mouth under the trim mustache was turned up in a smile.

Caroline shook her head, unable to speak. Her throat was closed from the dust and from the sudden rush of emotion. She felt herself swept into his arms, and she hugged Uncle Elisha back with all her might.

"And here is your aunt Jane," Uncle Elisha said, turning to reveal a small, plump lady in a yellow linen dress and matching bonnet.

"We were watching for a girl, and here you are a young lady," Aunt Jane said, smiling as she spoke. She took Caroline in her arms and kissed her on the cheek. "You look very much like your mother, my dear."

"Let's get out of this crowd," Uncle Elisha said, leading her and Aunt Jane to a handsome horse and buggy.

"My trunk!" Caroline suddenly remembered.

"Here it is!" The boy was there, grinning up at her. "Carried it from the coach I did, sir."

"All right then," Uncle Elisha said, reaching into his pocket and giving him a coin. The boy tipped his hat, then ran back into the crowd that still surrounded the stagecoach.

As Caroline was helped up onto the buggy seat, she looked back and saw that there were many boys, all about the same age, swarming around the stagecoach like summer flies on a cow. They were fighting over the bags and trunks that were being pitched down from the top of the stagecoach, and they were yelling at the tops of their lungs:

"Olson's Lodge! Your home away from home!"

"Freemont Hotel! No fleas in the beds. Guaranteed!"

"Newman Hall! Good food at good prices!"

"Frank House—German spoken!"

The voices began to fade as Uncle Elisha flicked the reins and sent the horse trotting down the crowded street.

"Now tell us, how was your journey, my dear?" Aunt Jane asked. "I do hope it was pleasant."

"It was fine, thank you," Caroline answered politely. She could never lie, but neither did she want to sound like she was complaining. "And thank you for coming to meet me," she remembered to add.

"You are quite welcome, of course," Uncle Elisha said. He smiled down at her warmly. After they had driven in silence for a moment, Uncle Elisha nodded to one side. "Ever seen this color brick before?" he asked. When Caroline shook her head he said, "It's called Milwaukee brick. The yellow color comes from the clay around these parts. It's becoming so popular, they're asking for it back east."

"'Tis a cheery color, is it not?" Aunt Jane asked.

Caroline nodded. It *was* a cheery color—it made the bustling street appear sunny and bright. As they drove, Caroline glanced one way and then the other. She knew her eyes must be round as saucers, but she couldn't help it. She had never in her life seen so many people all at once. The sidewalks seemed to swell with more and more bodies. Even the crowds at the State Fair years before had not seemed quite so daunting. Caroline glimpsed a few ladies in among the throngs of men. The ladies were dressed in beautiful silk dresses with matching parasols to shade them from the sun.

"How many people live here?" Caroline asked.

"Forty-five thousand at the last census," Uncle Elisha answered.

Forty-five thousand? Caroline could hardly hold that number inside her head, let alone imagine that many people living in one place! Her own little town of Concord had grown over the last few years, but still there were only about seven hundred fifty folks there.

"And we're getting bigger every day," Uncle Elisha continued. "I try to keep abreast of all the new developments in the newspaper, but it's not always easy. Change is happening at a breathtaking pace."

As if to prove his point, Uncle Elisha turned a corner and they rolled past several wooden skeletons of buildings under construction. Up and down the dusty street great teams of men were digging and lifting and hammering and sawing.

"New buildings going up by the hour, new roads being graded and paved," Uncle Elisha yelled over the noise.

The buggy wound its way around piles of lumber and brick. For a moment the dust whipped up by all the work became unbearable. Aunt Jane covered her face with her handkerchief, and Caroline hurried to do the same. With her eyes closed, Caroline listened to the shouts of the workers. Many different languages were being spoken. Suddenly

Caroline felt very far from Concord.

"Now we're clear of it," Uncle Elisha announced. "This is Main Street."

When Caroline opened her eyes, she saw that they were once more on a cobblestone street with shops on both sides. As she looked to her left, she glimpsed gigantic, crisp white sails gliding in between two tall buildings. She let out a little gasp. A great schooner was there beside them, and then it was gone again.

"The very biggest ships sail right up the Milwaukee River under our very noses," Uncle Elisha explained, noticing Caroline's reaction.

"Where do they go?" Caroline asked. She kept watching for the ship, but it had disappeared completely behind the row of buildings.

"They dock at the tanneries and breweries along the river and load up their cargo," Uncle Elisha said.

They continued down Main Street for several blocks. Caroline watched the swarm of people and the many shops with their bright signs and awnings. She felt herself wilting, tired from the overnight journey and suddenly overcome by all the new sights and sounds and smells. The city was noisy and bright, and in places the smell of fish and animals and other things Caroline could not identify was overpowering. She leaned back against the seat and touched the handkerchief to her brow.

"Don't worry," Aunt Jane said, seeming to sense what Caroline was feeling. She took Caroline's hand and patted it. "We're nearly home, my dear."

At the word "home," Caroline felt an ache. She thought of how often she had longed to really know what her mother's life had been like, coming from a city like Boston. Strangely, all she wanted to do at this moment was run back to the quiet woods, away from the noise and confusion. But she knew how much had been sacrificed for her to come to Milwaukee to go to school. Even if Mother and Pa had not said so, Caroline understood that they would be counting on the good wages she would bring in once she became a schoolteacher. And Caroline had made a promise to herself that she would not let her family down.

Modern Conveniences

Uncle Elisha turned onto a quiet, tree-lined street. Houses sat well back from the road, with sloping green lawns. Some of the homes were made of wood, and others were made of Milwaukee brick. Most were much bigger than Caroline's own home in Concord, with wide porches and lovely flower gardens.

"Corner of Cass and Lyon, that is where we reside," Uncle Elisha informed Caroline. He stopped the buggy in front of a neat square building made of Milwaukee brick.

Mother had said that Uncle Elisha had prospered in Milwaukee, and now Caroline could see for herself that this was true. Her uncle's home stood two stories high, with a high slanting roof. Caroline counted ten tall windows along the front and two square windows peeking out from the shingles. Two doors stood side by side, right in the center of the building. Both were painted a cheery red.

"Work and live in the same place," Uncle Elisha told Caroline as he tied the horse to a post and helped her from the buggy.

"Ah, the life of a newspaperman." Aunt Jane sighed, but she smiled too, so Caroline could tell she was only pretending to be exasperated.

Now Caroline could see that one of the red doors had a handsome brass knocker on it, and the other door had **MILWAUKEE WEEKLY REGISTER** and **QUINER'S PRINT SHOPPE** painted in fancy black lettering. That door opened and a tall young man came rushing out, wiping his hands on the long apron he was wearing.

"Hello, cousin!" he called, stopping in front

of Caroline and grinning down at her. He had sandy brown hair and brown eyes, and his face was familiar, but Caroline was not sure which cousin he was. "Don't worry," he said, laughing. "I hardly recognize you either. You were but a wee thing last time we visited your folks. And here you are now, quite the young lady."

"Now, William, stop embarrassing the poor girl," a lady's stern voice said from behind. Caroline knew this must be her cousin William, the oldest of Uncle Elisha's three sons.

"Oh, you're not embarrassed, are you, cousin?" William asked, grinning at her again. Caroline shook her head and smiled back at him.

The lady who had chided William came forward. She had dark hair that had begun to gray. Her face was long and thin, and her mouth turned down slightly, but her brown eyes were friendly. "Do you remember me, child?" she asked, holding out her hands for Caroline to take.

Caroline had a sudden sharp memory of three figures dressed in black stepping out of a wagon. Grandma, Uncle Elisha, and Aunt Margaret. That had been over ten years ago. A terrible day. The day the relatives had arrived to tell of Father's death. "You are Aunt Margaret."

"That is correct." Aunt Margaret smiled and leaned down to give Caroline a light kiss. "It is wonderful to see you after all this time."

"Well, then," Uncle Elisha said, suddenly appearing out of the door on the right. Caroline realized he had disappeared inside the house with her trunk. Now he was studying a gold watch he had pulled from his vest pocket.

"We know what that means, don't we, aunt?" William laughed again. He turned to wink at Caroline. "A tyrant is our boss! Keep the nose to the grindstone, that's his motto."

"Actually, as you should know by now, son, my motto is, 'Print the news while there's news to print,' which means we must be quick about our task." Uncle Elisha came forward and took Caroline's hand. "I do apologize, Caroline, but Mondays are always busy around the press. The *Register* is a weekly, don't you know? And that means it must be ready to go first thing Tuesday mornings."

"And that means no rest on Mondays for the poor lowly workers," William added.

"We will have plenty of time to get re-acquainted," Uncle Elisha said, patting Caroline's hand. "I am truly glad you have come to stay with us in Milwaukee, Caroline. I hope you will be happy here."

"Thank you, uncle," Caroline said shyly.

"Well then," Uncle Elisha said. "I leave you in capable hands." And with that he turned and went into the print shop.

"You must excuse your poor uncle," Aunt Jane said. "He gets quite caught up in his work."

"You are welcome to come in and see how we earn our keep," Aunt Margaret told Caroline.

"I wouldn't want to be in the way," Caroline said.

"Oh, never mind about that," Aunt Margaret replied. "Come along after you have settled in." She and William hurried back to the print shop.

"Does Aunt Margaret work in the newspaper office too?" Caroline asked in surprise as she followed Aunt Jane through the other door.

"Ah yes," Aunt Jane replied. "Your uncle is very forward thinking. He believes that ladies should work if they have a mind to. And he has trained several ladies in the business of printing. He says he prefers lady printers because they are apt to be on time and do not drink."

Caroline had never known much about Aunt Margaret, and she had never heard of ladies being printers. It sounded like an interesting profession, and it must be nice to work all together as a family. Over the years, Caroline had read Uncle Elisha's newspaper when he had sent copies along with his letters. Now she would be able to see for herself how a newspaper was printed.

"Shall I show you around before you freshen up?" Aunt Jane asked, stopping just inside a long hallway with buttery-yellow wallpaper and a brown woven carpet on the floor. Caroline noticed unusual lamps with glass globes attached to the walls and a staircase curving gracefully up to the floor above.

"Yes, please," Caroline answered. She was eager to see how her aunt and uncle lived.

"The dining room and kitchen are on this floor," Aunt Jane said, turning to open a set of double doors.

Inside the dining room, Caroline admired the cherry-wood table and chairs and the matching sideboard. The furniture was simple, but elegantly carved. Caroline wondered if it was all store-bought. When she was a little girl, Father had made their furniture, and now Pa and the boys made the things they needed. They did not have a dining room. Instead, the family ate at a large oak table in the middle of the kitchen.

Through another set of double doors, Aunt Jane's kitchen was large and tidy, with a fat iron cookstove, a wide brick fireplace, and a well-stocked pantry. There were also handy cabinets with glass fronts built right into one wall.

After the kitchen, Aunt Jane led Caroline back into the hallway and up the flight of stairs to the second floor.

"The parlor," Aunt Jane announced. "I spend much of my time here."

"Oh, I can see why," Caroline said.

The parlor was a lovely room with cabbage-rose print wallpaper, a rose-colored settee, and plush rose-colored chairs. Small framed paintings of flowers and fruit hung on the walls. Between the tall windows stood a square table with four matching chairs. The maroon-colored rug was thick and rich, and the delicate muslin curtains had been pulled back so that light streamed into the room, making everything sunny and cheerful.

"It is a beautiful home, Aunt Jane," Caroline said.

"Why thank you, my dear," Aunt Jane smiled. "Your uncle was lucky to have purchased this land when he did. And he bartered and traded for the material to build the house. We lived in a much smaller place until our second boy came along."

Caroline wondered what Aunt Jane meant about bartering and trading for the material, but she thought it might be rude to ask.

Aunt Jane quickly took her through the rest of the second floor. There were two handsome bedrooms, one for Aunt Jane and Uncle Elisha and one for the boys when they were young..

"Now my sons are all grown," Aunt Jane said sadly. "William has his own home nearby with his wife and son. And George Henry broke my heart by heading out west to seek his fortune. Johnny is the only one left, but we hardly ever see him. He clerks for a law office, and they keep him busy till all hours, poor boy."

Up yet another flight of stairs, Aunt Jane paused to catch her breath.

"Too much house for one old woman," she said, and sighed. "We may decide to let out the top floor next year. We've asked Aunt Margaret to share our home, but she has been renting rooms from a widow for some time, and she is quite settled now."

Caroline decided that Aunt Margaret must be very independent and modern to live on her own and work as a printer. It was strange that Grandma Quiner had never talked much about her only daughter. Aunt Margaret seemed to live an intriguing life.

"Now, let me show you to your room, my dear," Aunt Jane said. "I do hope you find it comfortable enough." She opened a door, and Caroline followed her inside.

The room was large and bright, with two wide windows to let the sun shine through. A desk and chair stood beside one of the windows, and a washstand with a china washbasin and an oval mirror hanging above it stood beside the other. Caroline's trunk had been left near a pine wardrobe and a chest of drawers. Nestled under a sloping ceiling, the plump bed was covered with a colorful windmill quilt.

Caroline felt something tightening in her chest as she looked at that bed. In all her life, she had never slept alone. For as long as she could remember, she had shared a bed with her sisters. She turned away because she did not want Aunt Jane to see that tears had welled up in her eyes.

Aunt Jane seemed to sense what Caroline was feeling. In a gentle voice she said, "This was your grandmother's room when she lived with us, Caroline. Sometimes I think I can still feel her here."

Now Caroline noticed the samplers hanging on the wall. They were ones that she and her sisters had done long ago and Grandma had taken with her to Milwaukee.

"Your grandmother spoke often of you and your sisters," Aunt Jane said. "She loved you a great deal."

"I miss her very much," Caroline managed to say. She realized that she was suddenly thinking of her father as well as her grandmother, two people she loved who were no longer among the living.

"So do I," Aunt Jane said. "Now I will leave you to rest and freshen up. Nora will be in to help you unpack as soon as she returns from the butcher."

Caroline wanted to ask who Nora was, but her aunt had already swept through the door and closed it behind her. Caroline stood for a moment in the quiet. After the cramped stagecoach and the ride through the busy streets and the quick introductions to her Milwaukee family, it felt good to be alone.

Slowly she removed her bonnet and gloves and placed them on the bed. Then she went to the desk and set her leather satchel upon it. She took out the things she had been told by the college to bring: four new notebooks, a primer, and a set of pens. One was the beautiful pen with the ivory tip shaped like a feather that her beloved teacher Miss May had given her four years ago. Caroline still had the little day journal she had received for her birthday back then, and she wrote in it from time to time.

With the sunlight pouring across it, the desk was a perfect place to write in her day journal and to do her schoolwork during the day. For evening work there was a lamp with a glass globe just like in the hallway, but Caroline could not figure out how it worked.

Crossing the room, Caroline stood in front of the washstand and glanced in the mirror. She did not look too rumpled from the trip. Her brown hair was smoothed back in a tidy bun. There was a tiny smudge of dirt under her chin, but the ribbons of her bonnet would have hidden that. She thought of how the man in the coach had called her a country girl, and her skin burned at the memory. She wondered if she looked so out of place here in the city but supposed the man had only called her that because she had told him she had never been to Milwaukee. Suddenly she remembered how the man had also called her pretty.

She leaned in and peered at herself more closely. Her round cheeks were flushed with color, and her eyes appeared large and very blue in her small face. She often thought that her nose was too long and her mouth was too wide. Now she wondered if she really was pretty.

Just then a sharp knock made her whirl around. A girl not much older than herself was standing in the doorway, her curly red hair under a white cap and a white apron over her dress.

"Och, I didna mean to startle you, miss!" The girl spoke in a thick Irish brogue. "I've brought some warm water for you, so you can wash the dust off yer face and hands. But the missus thought you might enjoy a bath as well. A terrible dirty ride I'm sure it was."

The girl bustled into the room and set a china pitcher of water upon the washstand next to the china washbasin. She stood for a moment, as if waiting for Caroline to say something, but Caroline was not sure what to say.

"Would you fancy a bath then, miss?" the girl asked.

"I don't know," Caroline replied uncertainly. Back home, they took baths only once a week on Saturday evenings.

"Well, I'll get one ready for you as soon as I unpack your trunk." The girl turned to inspect the trunk and then looked at Caroline expectantly. "If you just give me the key, miss, I will have this unpacked for you in a hurry."

"Oh!" Caroline said, fishing for the ribbon around her neck that held the key to the trunk. As she handed it over, it finally dawned on Caroline that this was Nora, and that Nora was a maid. Even seeing such a grand house, Caroline had never dreamed that her aunt and uncle would have a maid.

"My, how lovely these are!" Nora said, admiring Caroline's dresses as she hung them up in the wardrobe.

"Thank you," Caroline answered.

Besides the blue serge, Mother had made her two other dresses. Caroline could hardly believe it, and her sisters had been very jealous. But Mother had said she must not look out of place at college. One dress was made of a fine green wool and the other was a rich brown crepe with black fringe trim. Mother had used the money from selling eggs to buy the fabric, and she had copied all the patterns from *Godey's*.

"My mother made the dresses," Caroline told Nora, suddenly wanting to speak about her family. "She was a dressmaker back in Boston before she came west."

"Was she now?" Nora asked. "My own mother was a good seamstress, God rest her soul."

"Oh, I am sorry," Caroline said quickly, understanding that Nora meant that her mother had passed away. "Is your father still alive?"

"He has gone to his rest as well, miss. But your aunt and uncle have been like a mother and father to me, they have. Took me in when I came shivering off the boat from Ireland, they did, and gave me good honest work."

"Do you have any brothers or sisters?" Caroline asked. She could not imagine being totally alone in the world.

"Yes, I have one sister, and your aunt found her work as well. But now she is a married lady, and she and her husband took a claim outside the city."

"I have three sisters, and none of them are married yet," Caroline volunteered. "One of them is brand-new. Lottie. She is only one year old." Caroline was quiet, thinking of Lottie's beautiful blond curls and the way she opened her blue eyes wide when she was surprised by something. "I hope Lottie remembers me when I get home." Caroline sighed.

"Och, I'm certain she will," Nora said, smiling. "You never forget your own kith and kin."

Caroline stood quietly as Nora put away the rest of her things. She wasn't sure what else to do. Besides the new dresses, there was one everyday dress of sprigged calico, which had been Martha's before being reworked. Nora folded the new muslin shifts Caroline had sewn herself and the starched white petticoats, flannels, and wool stockings for the winter, and put them into the chest of drawers. The winter coat handed down from Martha and the knitted shawl and the other day bonnet went into the wardrobe. Finally, Nora put the three pairs of white gloves and four white handkerchiefs in a drawer and the one other pair of shoes under the bed. Caroline had never had so many clothes in all her life.

"There now!" Nora exclaimed when everything had been put away. "I'll take you down for a bath, if you're ready. And let's choose one of your other pretty dresses for changin' into so's I can clean the dress you've got on."

"All right," Caroline said uncertainly, choosing the brown crepe. As she followed Nora back downstairs, she wondered if she had heard correctly. Had Nora really said that she would clean the dress for her?

"Here we go," Nora announced.

They passed through the kitchen into a small windowless room. A large tin tub sat on the floor. Caroline waited for Nora to begin filling it with buckets of water from the kitchen. Instead Nora went to the tub and turned a little spigot. Caroline's mouth dropped open as water began to gush through the pipe into the tub. Nora let it run for a time and then tested it with her fingers.

"There we go—that should do nicely," she said. When she turned and caught sight of Caroline's expression, she let out a little laugh. "Go ahead, see for yourself, miss! The water is warm as warm can be."

Caroline reached out to test the water. She could hardly believe it. Not only was the tub filling itself, the water indeed was wonderfully warm.

"Don't ask me how it works!" Nora laughed. "Your uncle had a man come to rig it up just last month. Somehow the water goes into a contraption just outside this room and gets heated up. Hot water easy as you please! Same thing in the kitchen. A time-saver it is, believe me!"

Of course Caroline did believe Nora. She had spent her entire life hauling water from the river or the well and heating it over a fire or stove.

"All the modern conveniences, that's what your uncle likes," Nora said. "Like the gas. The city went to gas not so long ago, and not everybody wants it in their home. But your uncle wanted it right away."

"Gas?" Caroline asked.

"The lamps! They're gas!" Nora pointed to the glass globes Caroline had noticed throughout the house. "You turn the knob and the gas comes out! When you touch a bit of fire to it, the lamp lights up quick as you please! Your uncle swears it's safe, but it scares me to death. To think there are pipes running through this city, right under your very feet, carrying this strange thing called gas." Nora shook her head. "But it is another time-saver, I'll say that. A body doesn't have to go around filling oil lamps or trimming wicks. And the gas gives a wonderful bright glow, I must admit."

Caroline thought of all the hours she had spent making candles, a chore she hated because it was so time-consuming. And she thought of how she always had to squint to do her schoolwork in the evenings. Now she would be able to read well into the night and not worry about her eyes.

"Now then, I'll leave you to enjoy your bath." Nora said, turning off the water and leaving Caroline alone. "Just call out if you need me." She closed the door behind her.

Slowly Caroline undressed and got into the bath. The water was warm and clear. She had never in her life taken a bath in the middle of the day and without waiting her turn in the metal tub at home.

As she lay back and let herself relax, she thought of what Nora had said. All the modern conveniences. Lights and warm running water at the turn of a knob. She wasn't sure yet if she would ever get used to the bustle of the city, but she could certainly get used to these kinds of modern conveniences very easily.

Quiner's Print Shoppe

After she had bathed and rested, Caroline sat down to a quiet dinner with Aunt Jane. She had not eaten since early that morning, and she realized that she was very hungry. The tender beefsteak and boiled potatoes Nora had made were delicious.

"I dine by myself on Mondays generally," Aunt Jane said as they ate. "Your uncle rarely comes up before midnight, I am afraid."

Caroline wondered if her aunt was lonely, but she did not seem so. She told Caroline about the meetings she attended and the charity work she did.

"I go regularly to temperance meetings and abolitionist meetings. And I belong to the Ladies' Aid Society," Aunt Jane explained. "At the society, we make collections for the poor and work to improve the city in whatever way we can. At this time we are selling subscriptions to raise money for a lending library like they have back east."

"Oh, I thought there might already be a lending library here," Caroline said. She had read about lending libraries in *Godey's*. It was hard to imagine a whole building full of books that one could borrow without paying anything at all.

"Soon, very soon," Aunt Jane replied.

After they had eaten, Caroline wanted to offer to clear the dishes, but Nora bustled in and began to load everything onto a wooden tray.

"Would you like to go see the print shop now?" Aunt Jane asked Caroline. "I have a few things to attend to, and it's always interesting to see the newspaper as it's being printed."

"Yes, thank you," Caroline replied. She hovered for a moment longer beside the table, but Nora was too quick and efficient. She gave Caroline a wink as she carried the tray of dirty dishes back to the kitchen.

"Spend as much time as you like there," Aunt Jane said, seeing Caroline to the front door.

Outside, Caroline stood for a moment alone on the wooden sidewalk. A horseman trotted past, tipping his hat to her, and then a group of boys rushed by, their voices loud and their boots making a racket on the planks.

At first Caroline knocked softly at the print-shop door, but when no one answered, she turned the knob and went inside. The room was noisy and crowded with strange machines. The air was thick and warm with the sun streaming through the open windows, and there was an overwhelming smell of ink and paper. She saw her uncle and aunt and cousin and other men she did not know, but they were busy, and no one noticed her arrival. She decided to stand quietly near the door and watch the goings-on.

Two men stood at the largest of the machines. Both men wore white shirts with the sleeves rolled up above their elbows, long stiff aprons that went down below their knees, and round black hats with short brims. One man fed large sheets of paper onto a flat bed while the other man turned a hand crank that made several gears go round and round. The machine whirred and groaned as the men worked it.

William was working at a smaller machine. Behind him, Aunt Margaret sat on a tall stool at a long table that tilted up at an angle to meet the wall. Uncle Elisha stood at the back of the room, leaning over another man sitting at a roll-top desk.

"Come along now, Smitty!" Uncle Elisha's voice was loud above the noise of the machines. "We haven't got all day. You've been working on that story since morning."

"I'm going as fast as I can, Quiner," the man

retorted. "Some stories just can't be rushed if you want them to come out right."

"Well, of course I want it to come out right, Smitty, but I'd also like it to come out for this edition!" Uncle Elisha straightened up and caught sight of Caroline. "Ah, a visitor," he said, his face relaxing into a smile. "Come and I'll give you a tour, but watch yourself. Wouldn't want you to get ink on your pretty dress! Printing is a messy business."

Caroline made her way around the machines toward her uncle, holding her skirts close so as not to get them dirty.

"We're a two-press operation," Uncle Elisha explained, nodding to the two men at the big machine. "That's Mr. Ames and Mr. Johnson. They run the presses. Ames moves from town to town as the mood takes him. He's what we call an itinerant printer. We're lucky to have him a spell."

The men glanced at Caroline and gave quick smiles, but they did not stop their work. The gears continued to crank noisily, and the sheets of paper whooshed along the flat bed.

"We print handbills as well," he explained, heading over to the other machine. "William is printing them."

William grinned at Caroline but, just like the other men, did not slow down for an instant. Uncle Elisha took a square piece of paper from a tall stack beside William and showed it to Caroline. It was an advertisement for land in Kansas Territory.

FREE STATERS UNITE!
Land Is Rich and Plentiful!
Come to Kansas Territory
Right Now and Stake Your Claim!
Help to Ensure Another Free State
In Our Great Nation!

"We print handbills to pass out for the abolitionist cause," Uncle Elisha explained. "We're urging all able-bodied men to go to Kansas Territory. Trying to swing the balance so it's a free state, don't you know?"

Caroline did know a little bit about Kansas

Territory. Many people were going there to settle it, and there was a rush to see whether it would be a free state or a slave state.

"And here's where Maggie works," Uncle Elisha said, turning toward Aunt Margaret's desk.

Now Caroline saw that the desk was full of little wooden compartments. Aunt Margaret wore a long apron like the men, but she had not rolled up her sleeves. Instead, she wore little sleeves of gray cotton that went from her wrist to her elbow. She wore gloves as well, and the fingertips were stained with ink. As Caroline watched, Aunt Margaret's hands moved quickly back and forth from the wooden compartments to a metal plate in front of her.

"Maggie is the typesetter," Uncle Elisha explained. "All those little compartments are full of letters, and she has to line them up just so to form the words we print. She has more patience than most folks. I have tried to teach William, but he would have none of it."

"Women have more patience in life,

brother," Aunt Margaret said dryly, not looking up from her work.

"'Tis true, Maggie." Uncle Elisha laughed. "'Tis true." He turned and showed Caroline to another long table. "Here is where we keep all the previous year's editions of the *Register*." He picked one up and held it out for Caroline to see.

Under the bold heading **MILWAUKEE WEEKLY REGISTER** were seven fat columns of advertisements and various bits of news. Uncle Elisha flicked open the newspaper so Caroline could see that it was made up of four large sheets.

"We've grown by leaps and bounds over the past few years. We were only a one-sheet paper not so long ago," Uncle Elisha said. Then he patted a chair near the table. "Why don't you have a seat and read for a while? It might amuse you."

"I would enjoy that," Caroline said. Uncle Elisha left her at the table and headed to the back of the room, shouting out in a loud voice,

"Have you finished yet, Smitty?"

"Not quite, Quiner," the man called back.

"Why, you're as slow as molasses!" Uncle Elisha cried.

Caroline was surprised at how gruff Uncle Elisha sounded, but when she glanced back at the rolltop desk she saw that he was laughing at something Smitty had written. She decided that Uncle Elisha probably pretended to be cross to get things done.

Picking up an old edition of the *Register*, Caroline saw that the first page was made up entirely of advertisements. It appeared that one could buy anything at all in Milwaukee. Homes and property and furniture, the finest cloth, the finest lace, medicines to cure every ill, all manner of dry goods, fancy hats and ribbons and gloves, leather saddles and farm machinery and cows and chickens and horses. All the merchants promised the best items for the best prices anywhere. Caroline was particularly interested in the advertisements for fine ready-made dresses.

JUST IN! JUST IN!

You Are Invited to Come and
See with Your Own Eyes —
Finest Ready-Made Dresses
West of New York!
Satin and Lace!
The Very Latest Styles!

Back home in Concord, Mr. Jayson at the general store sold ready-made shirts for men, but Caroline had never seen ready-made dresses. How wonderful not to have to sew your own dress!

After the first page of advertisements, the rest of the newspaper was filled with articles about local events and politics. A new mayor named J. B. Cross had been elected the year before. Proposals for a new harbor had been approved. The state fair had been a success that year.

In addition to local news, there were reports on the goings-on in the rest of the country. A great deal had been written on the slavery issue.

Caroline became engrossed in a story about a runaway slave. The slave had escaped from the south and was being hidden in nearby Racine when his owner, accompanied by U.S. marshals, discovered him and tried to take him back. But a mob of Milwaukeeans had defended the slave, and he had been whisked away to Canada.

"Gripping stuff, eh?" William asked. He had come up behind her suddenly.

"Yes, it is," Caroline replied.

"We call that the Glover incident," William told her. "Joshua Glover is the name of the fugitive slave. Everybody's still up in arms about it 'round here on account of the trial in our U.S. District Court to imprison the men who helped. One of them is a Mr. Booth, who is an editor friend of Father's. Mr. Booth was found guilty and had to spend a month in jail and pay a thousand-dollar fine!" William shook his head in disgust. "We all feel pretty strongly about the slavery issue 'round here."

"So do I!" Caroline said quickly. "We have read the articles Uncle Elisha has sent us. Mother says slavery is a blight on our country."

"It is! I would go to Kansas Territory today

to join the Free Staters in their fight if I didn't have a wife and young son to think about. Bloody Kansas they're calling it now, because of all the fighting and bloodshed."

Caroline shuddered at the words. She could not imagine a place where there was so much violence the land was called "bloody."

"Who writes all the articles?" Caroline asked. She had noticed that the stories did not have anyone's name underneath the headlines. Instead, they were written by "A Concerned Citizen" or "A Young Abolitionist."

"Father and Mr. Smitty mostly, but I write a few myself," William said proudly. He pointed out some things he had written. "I am 'Young and Eager' and 'Raring to Go.' And if you want to know about fashionable events, I am 'Young Man About Town'!"

He pointed to a story about a boat race and how it was the event of the season.

"We all write under different names. That way it seems like there are more writers, and also it gets the public interested. Pulls them in right away." He held out a handwritten paper for Caroline to see. "This is my piece on horseback riding I just finished. I'm taking it to Aunt Margaret to typeset."

Caroline followed William to Aunt Margaret's desk. Aunt Margaret glanced over the article and began to assemble the letters as William went back to printing handbills. Aunt Margaret's hands flew back and forth from the wooden compartments that held each letter to the metal plate in front of her. Her fingers moved so quickly and expertly, Caroline could see why the job took patience. It was a lot like sewing—careful and exacting work.

In a little while, Mr. Ames came to collect what Aunt Margaret had typeset. She took a rest, straightening her back and stretching out her fingers. She seemed thoughtful for a moment, and then she gazed down at Caroline, her eyes sharp and inquisitive.

"I wonder how you will like it here in the city," she said.

"I don't know," Caroline answered honestly.

"Well, it is a wonderful opportunity to be able to study at a school started by Miss

STUTSMAN COUNTY LIBRARY
910 5TH ST S E.
JAMESTOWN, N D 58401

Catharine Beecher," Aunt Margaret said brusquely. "Do you know who she is?"

Caroline felt as if Aunt Margaret was a teacher who was expecting a right answer from her.

"Yes, I do," Caroline replied. "She has started other schools in the east, and she has written books. So has her sister. She wrote a book called *Uncle Tom's Cabin*."

Aunt Margaret nodded. "I do hope you will make the most of your schooling. We were pleased when Miss Beecher agreed to take over the female seminary here. Many of the finest families are sending their daughters to study at the college. It is quite something that you were accepted."

Caroline felt her stomach twist into a nervous knot at Aunt Margaret's words, and self-doubt was again back to plague her. What if she wasn't smart enough for this city school?

"Oh, stop bullying the poor girl, Maggie," Uncle Elisha cried, coming up beside them. "Caroline passed her examinations with flying colors, I hear." He gave an encouraging nod, and Caroline smiled gratefully up at him. His eyes crinkled just like she remembered Father's.

"Here is a poem to typeset," he said, showing it to Caroline first. "We like to print a poem a week. What do you think?"

Caroline quickly read through the poem.

Farm and City
Would you be strong? Go follow the plow:
Would you be thoughtful? Study fields and flowers;
Would you be wise? Take yourself a vow
To go to school in Nature's sunny bowers;
Flee from the city, nothing there can charm—
Seek wisdom, strength, and virtue on a farm.

"I like it," she said decisively, handing the poem back to her uncle.

"I thought you might," Uncle Elisha said, smiling again.

Aunt Margaret began to typeset the poem, and Caroline went back to reading past editions of the *Register*. As she read, men began to come in and out of the shop. Some brought work for Uncle Elisha to do, but others came to pick up their handbills. Instead of paying

Uncle Elisha in money, many of them brought goods to trade for the work.

Now Caroline understood what Aunt Jane had meant about Uncle Elisha bartering and trading for the material for the house. In no time, the front of the shop was crowded with burlap sacks of all manner of goods: cornmeal and flour and sugar and jars of honey and baskets of potatoes. Bartering and trading seemed to be how he ran his newspaper, and Caroline guessed that was how he had built his house.

“Do the men bring things every day?” Caroline asked Aunt Margaret when she had paused again in her work.

“They come at the end of each month,” Aunt Margaret replied. “That’s when payment is due for subscriptions or advertisements or handbills.”

One man even brought in a squealing piglet under one arm.

“I’m afraid my wife will never allow a pig into the house!” Uncle Elisha cried laughingly.

“Well, how ’bout I butcher ’im up for you then, sir?” the man asked.

"I would be much obliged," Uncle Elisha replied.

Another man told Uncle Elisha to come to his shop and pick out anything he wanted. "Biggest store in Germantown—in all of Milwaukee!" the man cried in a thick German accent.

At one point, a group of young boys came rushing in and stood by the door, waiting for Uncle Elisha. Their faces were dirty and their knickers had been patched many times. Uncle Elisha gave them all handbills about Kansas, and they went rushing out into the street, yelling at the top of their lungs, "Kansas Territory! Hurry up and pack your bags. Cheap land!"

"Those are the newsboys," Aunt Margaret explained to Caroline. "Elisha pays them to distribute the paper and to hand out the abolitionist bills as well. Most of them support an entire family on their wages, poor things."

Caroline thought of the boy who had taken her trunk that morning. He was most likely in the same situation as the newsboys. She was suddenly glad that Uncle Elisha had given him a coin.

As the afternoon wore on, more men came through the door and gathered in the back of the shop, near Uncle Elisha's desk. These men did not barter or trade. Instead, they pulled up chairs and sat and smoked pipes or large cigars and talked over the news of the day.

"Men call women gossips," Aunt Margaret said to Caroline in a low voice. "But I think it's the other way around. Those same men will come in here nearly every day to shoot the breeze."

"Are they newspapermen, too?" Caroline asked.

Aunt Margaret shook her head. "Doctors, lawyers, merchants and a few would-be politicians."

Caroline studied the circle of men more closely. They were all prosperous-looking in their well-made suits, striped vests, and colorful cravats.

Soon the air became smoky from the men's cigars and pipes. The room buzzed with conversation and the constant whirring of the presses. Caroline sat in the chair watching

Aunt Margaret's quick work and listening to the noise. She found all the hubbub strangely comforting, and her eyes began to grow heavy. She tried to keep them open, but before she knew it, she was being nudged gently awake. Nora was smiling down at her.

"The missus is almost ready for supper and asked me to come find you," Nora said.

"Supper already?" Caroline asked, stifling a yawn and glancing around. She was embarrassed that she had dozed for so long. The circle of men had left. Uncle Elisha, William, Aunt Margaret, and the other workers were all engrossed in their tasks.

Caroline followed Nora outside. The air had turned cooler, and they lingered on the wooden sidewalk for a moment. The sun was setting, and the street looked pretty in the fading light. Caroline caught sight of two men coming toward them carrying long poles. As they came closer, one of them tipped his hat.

"Howdee do, ladies?" he asked, giving them a wink.

"Hmmph!" Nora said under her breath.

"Howdee do, indeed." Nora frowned, but when the man who had winked turned back and grinned, Caroline could tell Nora was pleased.

"Who are those men?" Caroline whispered.

"Those are the lamplighters," Nora replied. "They go all through the town lightin' the lamps in the evenin' and turnin' them off again come mornin'."

The grinning lamplighter stopped at a tall lamppost on the corner and lifted his pole. Instantly a warm glow pulsed inside the glass globe.

"A star for you, darlin' ladies," he called out, and then gave a deep bow.

Nora made a *tsk tsk* sound, but then she laughed and smiled and the lamplighter smiled back.

"We should go in now," Nora said. But she stood with Caroline a moment longer, and they watched as the men went from lamp to lamp. All the way down the hill, the globes of light came on, little stars winking in the growing darkness.

Mah-au-wauk-seepe

"Milk! Fresh milk and cheese!"

"Eggs!"

"Potatoes! I have potatoes!"

"Fresh fish! Get yer fresh fish here!"

The voices mingled with Caroline's dreams until she awoke with a start. She was in a strange room, sleeping in a strange bed alone, without her sisters beside her. For a moment Caroline did not know where she was. Then she remembered. She was in Milwaukee, in Uncle Elisha's house.

"Bread! Nice fresh rolls. Hurry and get

'em while they're hot."

"Honey—sweet clover honey!"

Caroline lay back against the soft pillows, listening to all the unfamiliar sounds. Along with the voices, wagon wheels rattled and horses whinnied. The jingle of harnesses and the clip-clop of horseshoes rang over the cobblestones.

A new day had barely begun, and already the city sounded loud and busy. Caroline was used to rising early, but back home the morning sounds were soft and gentle—the rustle of her sisters waking up beside her, the murmur of her brothers' voices in the next room, the twittering of the birds in the trees. Here the world already seemed to be in a noisy rush.

"Read all about it!" a boy's voice called. "Get your newspapers here."

"Hot off the press!" another boy shouted. "*Milwaukee Weekly Register!* Come and get it!"

Caroline remembered the newsboys from the day before. She slipped out of bed and went to the window, moving the curtain aside just a little so she could peek outside without being seen.

Below, the street was alive with color and motion. Men dressed in work clothes were pushing brightly painted carts, calling out what they were selling at the top of their lungs. Caroline saw doors opening up and down the street, and ladies coming outside to buy from the hawkers. Most of the ladies wore dark dresses with large white aprons and white caps. Caroline realized that they were probably all maids. They called good morning to one another as they came outside.

The newsboys were standing in a little group right below her window. Several men in suits had stopped to purchase the *Register*. When the men left, the boys ran off, their voices fading as other voices took over.

"You call that fresh, Angus O'Leary?" a tall red-headed woman in a long white apron cried loudly. She stood with hands on hips before a bright blue cart with a green fish painted on the side. "I'm not certain it's the fish you should be callin' fresh."

There was laughter all around.

"This very fish was swimming in our great

lake only one hour ago," the man next to the fish cart replied. "You'll not find fresher unless you take a fishing pole yourself out onto the docks."

"I've caught a few fish in my time, I'll have you know," the woman replied.

"I'm sure you have, Mary McLean," the man chuckled. He made a great show of wrapping the large fish in a piece of brown paper. "I'll throw in a dozen clams to make it right between us."

"All right then," Mary McLean answered. She took the package and moved on to another cart, where she began to haggle over the price of eggs. Caroline guessed that haggling was expected when buying from the street hawkers. She noticed that all the other maids were doing the same thing. The chattering was like the humming of the cicadas in the woods at home—quietly insistent.

Somewhere a clock struck seven o'clock. Caroline knew she should get ready for breakfast, but she could not take her eyes off the scene below. It was mesmerizing, like watching the sights at a county fair. But after a time, the women went back into their houses and the hawkers moved on down the street.

"Good, you're up!" Nora came bustling in with a pitcher of water and Caroline's blue dress, fresh and clean.

"Oh, thank you, Nora," Caroline said, and she meant it with all her heart. She still could not believe that she would not have to clean her own dresses. She had a moment of guilt as she thought of her sister back home, and how she would have to do all the washing without her.

"You are quite welcome, miss." Nora hummed as she bustled about the room, making the bed and fluffing the pillows. Even though she liked Nora, Caroline felt a little self-conscious standing in her nightgown with a stranger. She went to the dresser and lifted the pitcher.

"My, this is heavy," Caroline commented. "It must be difficult to carry up all those stairs."

"Och, it would be, except that I dinna have

to!" Nora said. "There is a dumbwaiter in the wall."

"A dumbwaiter?" Caroline asked.

"'Tis a pulley contraption built straight into the wall. Works like a charm, it does. Carries anything you like straight up from the kitchen."

"Oh," Caroline said. She was going to ask to see the dumbwaiter, but Nora was already headed to the door.

"Breakfast is in the parlor this morning, miss." She paused. "It will do the missus good to have a young person around again. 'Tis a sad thing when the chicks leave the roost."

As she washed her face, Caroline thought about what Nora had said. At home, Joseph was the oldest, but she did not think he would be leaving yet. He liked farmwork and he had not yet become engaged to anyone. Henry would most likely be the first to leave, since he was always itching to travel. Suddenly Caroline was struck by how strange it was that she was the one to go away on this adventure, when it was Henry who was always yearning to see new places.

After she had washed, Caroline looked at her blue serge. It was spotless and crisp. She decided to hang it up in the wardrobe and put on the brown crepe again. It was wonderful to have a choice of dresses. She remembered a time not so long ago when she had had only one dress to wear every single day.

Down one flight of stairs, Caroline found her aunt and uncle in the parlor. They were sitting at the table, which had a lace cloth covering it. Uncle Elisha had the newspaper open before him, but he folded it when he saw Caroline.

"Good morning!" his voice boomed.

"I hope you slept well, my dear," Aunt Jane said.

"Oh yes, thank you," Caroline replied.

"Good, good," Uncle Elisha said. "Now dig in while it's hot."

There were boiled eggs in little china eggcups and warm rolls with butter and honey. And there was good strong coffee to drink. Caroline had not seen Nora outside, but she wondered if anything on the table had been purchased from the hawkers.

Uncle Elisha cleared his throat and asked Caroline to tell him about the farm. "It must be greatly improved since I saw it last."

"Yes, it is," Caroline replied. "Pa and the boys have cleared most of the land now. We have fields of wheat and oats and barley."

"What about the drought?" Uncle Elisha asked. "The whole state has been hard hit these past two years."

Caroline nodded. They had had two wonderful years, and then everything had dried up. The last two years, the crops had suffered a great deal. "It has been difficult, but Pa says next year is sure to be better," Caroline said.

"Let us hope so." Uncle Elisha smiled. "The life of a farmer is hard indeed. No one can predict the future."

Talking of the hardships on the farm made Caroline think once more of the great expense of sending her to college. She bit her lip and looked down at her plate.

"Now take a look at this!" Uncle Elisha said. He flicked open the newspaper and proudly held it out for Caroline to see. "Hot off the press, as we say in the trade."

Caroline glanced over the columns. She saw the lines of poetry her aunt had typeset the day before and also the report on horse riding from "Young Man About Town."

"Riding sidesaddle as a pastime is bound to go among the ladies," the article read. "It is all the rage back east, and the ladies of this fair little city by the lake are determined never to be far behind their eastern sisters."

"So, what do you think of our newspaper?" Uncle Elisha asked, his eyes twinkling.

Caroline thought for a moment. "I think it's thrilling to hear about the news one day and see it printed the next," she replied.

"Well put, my dear! Well put!" Uncle Elisha patted Caroline's hand, then checked his pocket watch.

"Now Elisha, what is the hurry this morning?" Aunt Jane asked.

Uncle Elisha snapped his watch closed and smiled fondly at his wife. "I do hate to leave such wonderful company, but I am afraid I must." He turned to Caroline. "Tuesdays are not quite as busy, once the paper is out, but a newspaperman never rests. So much is going on in this city. Right now I have an appointment to discuss the new harbor that's in the works. Our city officials hope to have it completed in record time. But there's still a lot of digging and planning to do, and I must keep our readers abreast of the developments."

"Goodness, our city officials are always in a stir to move heaven and earth as they see fit," Aunt Jane said, shaking her head.

"Well, there wouldn't be much of a city if some moving had not been done," Uncle Elisha countered. "Did you know, Caroline, that not so very long ago, much of this city was but a swamp? It took some gumption to build the city up from marshland. There has been a great deal of digging and filling in and grading. It is quite something! This is a man-made city, and I must admit I am proud of the fact."

Uncle Elisha kissed his wife on the forehead and took his leave. Caroline stood to help Aunt Jane put the breakfast things on a silver tray.

"Do not trouble yourself, my dear," Aunt

Jane said. She took the tray to a little hidden cupboard in the wall Caroline had not noticed before.

"Is that the dumbwaiter?" Caroline asked.

"Yes it is," Aunt Jane replied. "Would you like to see? It's very handy." She pulled on a little lever, and the tray disappeared from sight. "It goes straight down to Nora in the kitchen."

Now that breakfast was over, Caroline wondered what would happen. At home by this time, she would have already fed the chickens and geese and helped put the dishes away after the meal and gotten ready for school. But college did not start until next week, and Caroline wondered if there were any chores to do in her aunt and uncle's home. It seemed strange not to have any work to do.

"Idle hands are the devil's playthings," Mother always said.

"I could help Nora with the cooking," Caroline suddenly blurted. "And I could do some chores."

Aunt Jane smiled. "I know it will take some

getting used to, living here with us. You will be quite busy when school begins on Monday."

And Caroline knew that to be true. Part of her yearned for Monday morning to arrive and part of her dreaded it. Her stomach twisted nervously each time she tried to envision her first day surrounded by strangers.

A loud knocking was heard from below, startling Aunt Jane. "Oh, goodness, who could that be at this hour?" she asked. She peered at a mirror just outside the window. Caroline could see that it was set at such an angle that one could see who was standing at the door below without being seen.

"Oh, how nice, it's Alice and Billy!" Aunt Jane cried happily.

Caroline heard Nora opening the door below, and the sound of greetings, and then a young voice was calling, "Grandma, Grandma!"

In a moment a little boy came charging through the door. He had blond hair and pink chubby cheeks and looked to be about three or so. He stopped when he saw Caroline and shyly put his thumb in his mouth and stared at her with big blue eyes. In a moment a pretty young woman appeared behind him.

"This is William's wife, Alice," Aunt Jane said, "and this is my pride and joy, little Billy."

"We had to meet the new arrival!" Alice said, taking off her yellow bonnet. She was very fair, with blond curls and blue eyes.

Nora bustled in and took a teapot and teacups and milk and sugar out of the dumbwaiter and set them before Aunt Jane on the table. She gave two rolls to Billy, and he grinned up at her and began to devour them.

"Oh thank you, Nora," Alice said. "Our little Billy will eat us out of house and home!" She leaned down and said something to Billy in a language Caroline did not recognize. Billy swallowed his mouthful of roll and replied in the same language, and then began to eat more slowly.

"We're speaking Finnish," Alice explained when she caught sight of Caroline's confused expression. "I am from Finland, you see. My parents came here when I was just a little baby, but we still speak the old language at home, and I speak it to Billy."

"Does William speak Finnish too?" Caroline asked.

"Well, he has learned a little," Alice replied, chuckling. "But it's handy to speak a different language when one wants to keep secrets from one's husband!"

Caroline glanced at Aunt Jane wondering what she would think about keeping secrets from William, but she looked amused. Caroline could tell the two women got along very well.

"Isn't it fun to meet new family?" Alice cried, reaching out to squeeze Caroline's hand. "I think we will be good friends."

"I think so too," Caroline replied. It *was* fun to meet new family. If she had not come to Milwaukee, she might never have met William's lovely wife and sweet little boy.

For the rest of the morning, Caroline played with Billy while Alice and Aunt Jane took out their knitting and chatted. With his blond curls and blue eyes, Billy reminded Caroline of Lottie, and somehow being with him made her feel closer to her little sister.

Billy brought out a spinning top from his pocket to show Caroline. "Grandpa made it for me," he said, crouching down and winding a piece of string around the wooden top. He pulled the string, and the top spun across the floor. "You try it now!" he commanded Caroline.

"Now, don't let Billy wear you out," Alice told Caroline in a firm voice.

"Oh, he won't!" Caroline replied. Since there seemed to be no chores to do around Aunt Jane's home, minding Billy made Caroline feel useful.

The morning went by quickly, and soon Nora was calling them all down to dinner. The table was already set, and Nora had made a roast chicken with creamed carrots. It was Caroline's fourth meal in the house, and she still felt strange being waited upon.

After dinner, they went outside so that Billy could run about. Caroline had not realized Aunt Jane kept a garden just behind the house.

"Not so big as your garden back home, I'm sure," Aunt Jane said.

Caroline looked around at all the beautiful flowers. Back home they did not grow any flowers at all. Their garden was meant to feed them for the whole year. She knew her brothers and sisters would be harvesting the fall vegetables soon.

After Alice and Billy left, Aunt Jane said that she needed a little rest herself, and so she went upstairs to her bedroom. Caroline thought about going to the print shop, but she decided to go to her own room instead. Perhaps she would start a letter home. She had been gone only two days, but she had already seen so much.

Inside her room, she stood at one of the windows for a moment. Several of the women she had seen early that morning were outside again. Now they were cleaning the wooden steps leading up to the front doors of their houses. They carried buckets and rags and worked at the steps until they gleamed in the sun. A few of them chatted, and one of them was humming as she worked. Her voice was lovely, lilting out a melancholy tune Caroline had never heard before.

Caroline sat down at the desk and started a letter home. She wrote a little bit about the stagecoach journey, but she did not mention the cramped seats or the drunken men. She told all about seeing the newspaper being printed and about Alice and Billy. She had written nearly a whole page in careful tight script when there was a knock at the door. It was Aunt Jane.

"I like to walk to the lake before supper. I thought you might care to join me?"

Caroline put on her bonnet and followed Aunt Jane outside. The air had turned a little cooler, since the sun was going down, and a nice breeze was blowing.

"Is it always so warm?" Caroline asked.

Aunt Jane nodded. "Unfortunately, yes, during this time of year. But winter always sneaks up on us. In a few weeks it will be rainy and cold. And very soon we'll be iced in altogether. The lake and the river freeze, and no ships can get in or out."

As they walked, they passed other ladies out strolling and gentlemen coming home from work. Aunt Jane nodded and said, "Good day," to everyone.

In the alleyways between the houses, bands of boys were playing marbles or tag. Some were rolling wooden hoops down the street.

When they came to the end of the street, Aunt Jane turned right and the land sloped downward. The wind grew stronger and blew at their skirts and the ribbons on their bonnets. There was a wetness in the air, and the loud, high cawing of birds could be heard in the distance. Up ahead, a patchwork of color fluttered against the blue sky.

"Boys come here to fly their kites," Aunt Jane explained.

It was such a pretty sight, all the kites soaring and diving, that Caroline wished Thomas were here. How he would enjoy flying a kite.

Aunt Jane led the way up a grassy bluff in among the boys, and then she stopped. "Lake Michigan in all her glory," she said.

Caroline could only stare wide-eyed at the sight before her. Nothing had prepared her for the largeness of the lake. It stretched out as far as she could see, a vast field of gray-blue melting into the deeper blue of the sky. Overhead, white birds flew, dipping down to catch fish in their long beaks. Great schooners with tall white sails moved effortlessly across the water.

As Caroline watched the schooners, she found herself thinking about her father. He had crossed this very body of water many times on his trading expeditions. Perhaps on his final voyage, he had set off on a day like this one, the waters calm, a gentle breeze in the air. How could he have known that the winds would change and a terrible storm would capsize his ship? How could he have known that he would never see his wife or his children again?

Caroline felt a chill run through her. She closed her eyes and tried to see her father, tall and strong, on the deck of a schooner, but she realized that her memories of him had faded over the years. When she tried to picture him, she saw Uncle Elisha's face instead, and this made her sad. She opened her eyes again.

Aunt Jane had walked a little way ahead, and

Caroline moved to follow. They strolled along the bluff in silence for a time, and then Aunt Jane spoke; she seemed to be quoting something:

> *"Below me roar the rocking pines,*
> *Before me spreads the lake*
> *Whose long and solemn-sounding waves*
> *Against the sunset break."*

"That's pretty," Caroline said.

Aunt Jane nodded. "Lines from the poet John Greenleaf Whittier. He was writing about another of our great lakes, but it doesn't matter. An inspiring sight, is it not?"

"Yes, it is," Caroline replied. "I didn't know it would be so very . . . big."

"It reminds me of home," Aunt Jane said. "I used to be able to see the ocean from where I lived when I was a girl."

Caroline remembered that Aunt Jane had come from Boston with Uncle Elisha. She and Mother had known each other a little when they were girls.

"Do you ever miss the east?" Caroline asked.

"Yes, but it is exciting here. We have watched this place grow from a rough trading settlement into a city in such a short time. It has not always been pleasant, but it is never dull."

Caroline told her about the men on the stagecoach stating that they felt Milwaukee should be crowned the "Queen of the Lake."

Aunt Jane looked thoughtful for a moment. "Sometimes I think our city is more like a gypsy than a queen. But 'tis true we might rival even Chicago soon enough."

They turned and began walking back the way they had come. Aunt Jane continued speaking. "The name of Milwaukee comes from the Powawatomi, the Indian tribe that used to live here. Mah-au-wauk-seepe was the original name. It means a 'gathering place of rivers.' It is a perfect name because it has also become a gathering place for all kinds of people from many different countries."

Caroline remembered the different languages she had heard spoken the day before as

Uncle Elisha drove through the city streets. She thought of how Alice had been born in another country but now she was an American, and so was her son.

When they reached the boys with their kites, Caroline stopped to take a final look at the lake before leaving the bluff. The sun had just set, and the lake was not shimmering anymore. It seemed dark and cold and forbidding, and once more Caroline thought of her father and felt a chill run through her. She turned and followed Aunt Jane home.

Turtle Soup

The next morning Aunt Jane and Caroline walked to a busy outdoor market not far from the house.

"All the farmers from outside the city bring their goods to sell here each Wednesday," Aunt Jane explained.

The market took up two whole city blocks. Stalls with colorful awnings lined the sidewalks, and rough country wagons stood in the center of the street. Many of the farmers called out their wares, just like the hawkers did in the morning under Caroline's window.

"Get your apples here! Apples and fresh cider!"

"Sweet corn! Beautiful sweet corn!"

Aunt Jane carried a basket over one arm. She stopped to buy a dozen rosy apples and a dozen ears of corn. She inspected cabbages and yellow squash and round green melons. Sometimes she haggled with the farmers until they brought their prices down a little.

"As you've noticed, we receive many goods from your uncle's customers," Aunt Jane told Caroline as they strolled, "but I still need to do the marketing for the fresh produce."

While she waited for Aunt Jane to buy some green beans, Caroline lingered in front of a wagon with chickens clucking in wooden cages and eggs carefully packed in crates.

"Would you fancy some fresh eggs, miss?" a red-faced farmer's wife asked Caroline, wiping her hands with the apron she wore. "Just laid this morning."

Caroline shook her head. In her nice clothes, she knew she must look like all the other city folk out doing their marketing, but it felt strange to be called "miss" by this woman. Caroline had an urge to tell the farmer's wife that she herself kept chickens at home and that she sold the eggs to the general store, but the woman had turned away to help a customer.

"Ah, lemons!" Aunt Jane said, stopping at a stall with bright yellow lemons stacked in a pyramid. She picked one up and sniffed it and held it out for Caroline to do the same.

Caroline breathed in the sharp, sunny scent, and it made her mouth water. She could not remember the last time she'd had lemonade. It was such a rare treat. Mr. Jayson at the general store in Concord hardly ever had any lemons, and even when he did, they were much too expensive for every day.

Aunt Jane carefully chose four lemons and paid the man at the stall. Then she glanced down at her basket.

"I think that should do," she said, tucking a calico cloth over her goods.

They strolled slowly back through the maze of wagons and carts. Caroline glimpsed a butcher's stall and a baker's stall and a woman selling herbs from a small cart. On the raised plank sidewalk, a man was playing a fiddle. A small circle of folks had gathered around him.

"He's a street performer," Aunt Jane told Caroline as they stopped to listen. "He plays for money."

The man played "Billy Boy" and "Pop! Goes the Weasel. " When he paused, a small boy darted in among the listeners. The boy held out a hat, and several people dropped coins into it, including Aunt Jane. The boy nodded his thanks. Caroline wondered how much the fiddler made in a day.

After the market, Aunt Jane had a few more errands to do. They stopped at Gentry's Men's Shop to pick up two new shirts for Uncle Elisha and at the cobbler's to collect a pair of Uncle Elisha's boots that had been resoled. Caroline carried the boots and shirts, wrapped up in brown paper and tied with string, for her aunt as they continued down the sidewalk.

Buggies and horses clattered by on the cobblestone street. Caroline noticed a long wagon stopped at the corner. It was built something like a stagecoach, with walls and a roof overhead. Many faces peered out from the side windows, and more riders clambered up the steps.

"That is an omnibus," Aunt Jane said. "A person can pay a fare and ride to different parts of the city."

As they walked, Caroline began to notice a strong yeasty odor permeating the air. It was as if a great deal of bread was being baked all at once.

"'Tis the beer being brewed," Aunt Jane explained. "The breweries are on the other side of the river, carved into the bluffs, but the odor sometimes clouds the entire city." Aunt Jane gave a little sigh. "Do you know about the Temperance Society?"

"Grandma told me about it when she used to visit," Caroline replied. "And I've read a little about it. The Temperance Society tries to get folks to stop drinking liquor."

"That is true," Aunt Jane said. "We also work to persuade officials to pass laws that will stop liquor from being made or sold at all.

That is what they did in the state of Maine. They made it illegal to brew spirits of any kind. We're hoping to pass a similar law here. It is going to be a struggle, however. The brewers are powerful businessmen in our city."

Aunt Jane paused when they came to an alleyway between the tall buildings. "Now then, I thought we might have an early dinner," she said. "How would you like to go to a restaurant as a special treat?"

"Oh," Caroline said, thoughts rushing around inside her head. She had heard of restaurants, of course, but she had never been to one. The stagecoach had stopped at an inn so that the passengers could have breakfast. Mother had packed bread and fresh butter for the journey, and Caroline had sat outside the inn under a tree waiting for the stagecoach driver to feed and water the horses.

"A restaurant must be very expensive," Caroline said in a small voice. Mother had given her spending money, but it was meant to last the whole nine months in Milwaukee.

"Do not worry, my dear," Aunt Jane said, waving a hand in the air. "We told your mother we would look after you while you were with us, and that is what we intend to do."

Aunt Jane tucked Caroline's arm under her own and led her down the alleyway. They stopped in front of a door with a sign hanging over it.

BILLINGTON RESTAURANT

GOOD FOOD SERVED DAILY

"This is one of my favorite restaurants in the city," Aunt Jane said. "The food is simple, but good."

A gentleman coming out of the door held it open for them, tipping his hat as Aunt Jane and Caroline passed through. Inside, the restaurant was small and square, with a low ceiling criss-crossed by dark mahogany beams. Nicely dressed ladies and gentlemen sat at round mahogany tables eating from white china plate and bowls. The room was abuzz with voices and the clatter of dishes. Caroline's mouth watered as delicious smells wafted through the air.

"Good afternoon, ladies." A tall man in a dark suit appeared and gave a quick bow. "Two for dinner?"

"Yes, please," Aunt Jane answered.

"Shall I hold your packages?" the man asked.

"That would be nice, thank you." Aunt Jane gave the man the basket and Caroline handed over the parcels. The man set them on a shelf near the door with some other packages.

"Right this way, ladies," he said, turning on his heel.

Aunt Jane and Caroline followed him to a table in the corner. The man helped them into their seats, then placed two sheets of thick parchment on the table beside white linen napkins. He bowed again and departed.

Aunt Jane removed her gloves, laid them neatly on the table, and then took the napkin and placed it on her lap. Caroline quickly did the same.

"These are the menus," Aunt Jane explained. "There are always several items to choose from."

Caroline looked down at the menu.

Codfish Balls and Sauce
Fishermen's Stew
Fried Trout
Shepherd's Pie
Turtle Soup

Meals are $1.00.
Served with bread, and tea or coffee.

All the good smells were making Caroline's stomach rumble. She glanced sideways at a large plate of food on a nearby table. From what Caroline could see, the portion looked hearty. Still, a dollar was a lot of money to pay for one meal. Aunt Jane did not seem to be bothered by the price, however.

"Please choose whatever you wish, my dear," she said. "What I enjoy about going to restaurants is being able to sample dishes one wouldn't normally eat. The turtle soup, for instance. It is a specialty here, and it is quite tasty."

Caroline studied the menu again. She had had codfish and trout and shepherd's pie. But she had never had a fisherman's stew or turtle soup.

"Have you decided, ladies?" The man who had seated them had returned.

"A bowl of the turtle soup, please," Aunt Jane said.

"And for you, miss?" The man turned to Caroline.

Caroline hesitated. "I will have the turtle soup, too," she said at last.

"Very well." The man took up their menus and walked away.

Caroline glanced about the room again. A young serving girl wearing a starched white apron and cap was winding her way between the tables toward the back of the restaurant, an enormous tray laden with dirty dishes hoisted high upon one shoulder. More customers were arriving, and the man in the black suit was busy seating them all. Gentlemen removed their hats as they entered, but ladies kept their stylish bonnets on their heads. Many bonnets were fancy with lace and velvet trimmings. One lady even had tulle wrapped around her straw bonnet so it looked like a bird's nest. When she came closer, Caroline saw there was actually a little stuffed wren sitting right in the middle of the nest.

"Ah, here we are," Aunt Jane said, as one of the serving girls arrived with two steaming bowls of soup, a dish of sliced hard-boiled egg, and a plate of crusty bread, thickly sliced.

The soup was dark and thick and gave off a strong, salty aroma. Caroline picked up her spoon and dipped it into the bowl, stirring up potatoes and carrots and onions and thick chunks of turtle meat. When the soup was cool enough to taste, she decided it was like a rich beef broth, only tangier and saltier.

"So, what do you think?" Aunt Jane asked.

"The soup is delicious," Caroline answered. "Thank you so much for bringing me here, Aunt Jane."

"My pleasure, my dear," Aunt Jane said. "Now eat up!"

Caroline noticed that Aunt Jane was putting the round slices of hard-boiled egg into her soup as a garnish, and she did the same. The crusty bread was fresh and warm and perfect for dipping into the thick broth.

Caroline was quiet, savoring every spoonful of the tasty soup. As she ate, her thoughts suddenly turned to her family in Concord. At this very moment, she knew, Mother and Martha would be setting the table for their own dinner, getting ready for Pa and the boys to come in from the fields. Eliza and Thomas would be in the school yard, eating from the dinner pail packed from home. Caroline could picture exactly what they were all doing, but she knew they would never be able to guess what she was doing: sitting in a restaurant, eating turtle soup.

Up and Doing

The rest of the week went quickly by. In the mornings Caroline went with Aunt Jane as she did her errands about town. In the afternoons she sat in the print shop, reading past editions of the *Register*, chatting with Aunt Margaret, and listening to the voices from the back of the room. Caroline realized that sitting in a newspaper office was a good way to learn about the city.

Each day the same men wandered into the shop and gathered around Uncle Elisha's desk. They drank the coffee Uncle Elisha kept going on the potbellied stove, and they smoked their cigars or pipes and talked over the news of the day.

"There's a new hotel going up on Michigan and Broadway, built by a rich fellow named Newhall. Aims to be the best hotel west of New York."

"The railroad line to Chicago will be finished this spring. Now we'll be able to ride the cars down there in no time flat."

"You'll be able to go anywhere in this great country in no time flat, mark my words. There will be railroad tracks crisscrossing the whole nation one day, I'll wager."

"Another boatload of emigrants arrived in the harbor last night. Another three hundred souls seeking their fortune on our fair shores."

"I heard fifteen men were locked up last night for being drunk and disorderly."

"Sad to hear, but at least this new police brigade is doing the job the mayor pays them for."

Caroline looked questioningly at Aunt Margaret, who frowned at this last bit of news.

She said to Caroline in a quiet voice, "I don't want you to be fearful, but there have been an increasing number of robberies and fights in our city due to drinking. Now the mayor has formed a special brigade of policemen to keep order."

Caroline was alarmed to think of the city needing a special brigade for safety.

"I am convinced that if we could close down the breweries and the inns and taverns, we wouldn't need the police at all," Aunt Margaret continued. "There are beer gardens all over the city now."

"Beer gardens?" Caroline asked. She had never heard of such a thing.

"Yes. It is a German custom, I believe," Aunt Margaret answered. "The Germans have opened many outdoor cafés where they sit and drink beer in the open air, even on a Sunday."

"Even on a Sunday?" Caroline repeated, shocked. She knew that drinking liquor was wrong, and it must be especially wrong to do it on the Lord's day.

"Yes, but if the Maine Law passes, we won't

have to worry about such things anymore," Aunt Margaret replied.

"Aunt Jane told me about the temperance meetings you both attend," Caroline said.

Aunt Margaret nodded. "Perhaps you will come with us to the next meeting."

It sounded like a command rather than a question, and Aunt Margaret did not wait for a response before she informed Caroline that she should also attend abolitionist meetings.

"Young ladies should not hide behind their skirts and feign ignorance to what is going on in this country," she said. "We must rise up and help our brothers in the fight to abolish slavery."

Of course Caroline agreed with Aunt Margaret about drinking and slavery, but she found Aunt Margaret's direct way of speaking a little hard to get used to. It was funny that Uncle Elisha called his sister Maggie, when she seemed so much like a Margaret to Caroline with her gruff manner.

"Never been married," Aunt Margaret proclaimed. "Never wanted to be married. Never wanted a husband to tell me what to do."

Caroline couldn't help but giggle at Aunt Margaret's words. She had never heard a lady say such a thing. Most girls she knew hated the idea of being old maids.

"Now, Mother tried to marry me off several times when I was a young thing, but I never would let her do it," Aunt Margaret continued. "Gave her fits, I'm afraid. Never did approve of me working in the print shop." Aunt Margaret sighed. "But you can't live your life to please others—that's what I have learned."

Perhaps this was why Grandma Quiner had never spoken much about her only daughter, Caroline thought to herself. Grandma had not liked the idea of Aunt Margaret working, even if it was with Uncle Elisha.

"I believe a woman should be able to support herself if she has a mind to," Aunt Margaret continued. "I approve of you for wanting to be a schoolteacher." She looked down at Caroline with her piercing gaze. "Maybe we're cut from the same cloth."

Caroline smiled and nodded to be polite.

She was glad that her aunt approved of her, but deep down she did not really think they were alike. Caroline wanted to be a schoolteacher because she loved school and because she knew she could help her family with her wages. But she did not think she would always be a schoolteacher. One day she hoped to have a husband and children and a home of her own.

Nevertheless, Caroline did not want to disappoint her aunt, and so she made a point of asking when the next meetings were.

"Well, we don't have an abolitionist meeting scheduled for a while, but there's a temperance meeting Friday evening," Aunt Margaret said.

And so on Friday evening after supper, Caroline went to her first temperance meeting. Uncle Elisha drove, and they picked up Aunt Margaret on the way. The house Aunt Margaret lived in was not very far away, on the corner of Eighth and Sycamore streets. It was a simple two-story wood-frame house with bright red geraniums growing in boxes at the windows.

"Good evening all!" Aunt Margaret called as

she came out the door. "Here we go to fight the good fight!" She turned to Caroline after she had settled into the buggy. "And I'm glad we have a new soldier to join us."

Caroline wasn't sure she wanted to be a soldier, but she smiled back at Aunt Margaret anyway. Uncle Elisha drove through the darkening streets. Caroline saw the lamplighters and the shopkeepers closing the shutters and locking the doors of their shops.

"There are two of the policemen I told you about," Aunt Margaret said, nodding toward two young men standing on the corner. They were dressed in matching blue suits with shiny brass buttons running down the front and blue caps.

The buggy turned down Biddle Street, and they drove past rows of houses all bunched together with tall steps leading up to the doorways. Caroline was surprised to see whole families gathered on the steps, sitting and chatting and watching the passersby. Small children played on the sidewalks, and babies were tucked in mothers' arms.

"It's such a warm evening, everyone wants

to be outside to catch any kind of breeze," Aunt Jane remarked.

As they passed, Caroline wondered what it would be like to live on such a street crowded with houses and people right next door. It seemed like a friendly way to live, so close together.

Uncle Elisha drove around a pretty little square where the courthouse sat on one corner. Then they stopped in front of a large church made of Milwaukee brick with a tall steeple and beautiful stained-glass windows.

"This is our own congregation," Aunt Jane told Caroline.

"The temperance meetings are in churches," Aunt Margaret explained. "That way no one can criticize us for organizing."

Caroline was not sure what Aunt Margaret meant, and her aunt must have seen her confusion, because she said, "Many men think that the temperance league is about women's rights, not about temperance. When we meet in churches, it shows that we have the approval of our ministers and our community."

Caroline followed the aunts into the church while Uncle Elisha parked the buggy. Inside the church there were about twenty-five ladies and a handful of gentlemen milling about. Aunt Jane introduced Caroline to a few of the ladies, and then they took their seats on a carved mahogany pew. Uncle Elisha joined them just as the meeting began.

A lady in the front pew stood up and said importantly, "I call this meeting of the Milwaukee Temperance League to order."

Then another lady stood and made her way to the pulpit. She wore a plain brown dress, and her gray hair was pulled back in a severe knot.

"We shall review the minutes of the last meeting and then move on to current business," the lady announced.

"That is the secretary of the league, Mrs. Walker," Aunt Jane whispered to Caroline.

"We agreed to form a committee to meet with Mayor Cross to discuss the need to pass our own version of the Maine Law." Mrs. Walker consulted a list and read the names of the committee members. Caroline felt proud to hear her aunts' names among them.

"Now I shall hand the meeting over to Reverend Whitley," Mrs. Walker said, after she had given the time and place for the committee to meet.

A minister took his place at the pulpit and gave a long, rousing sermon on the evils of "demon rum." After that there was some hymn singing. Caroline decided that temperance meetings were a little like going to church on Sunday.

When the singing was over, a lady named Mrs. Ostrander stood and addressed the crowd. Aunt Jane whispered that she was the president of the Wisconsin Woman's State Temperance Society.

"Many men believe we should stay home and mind our own business." Mrs. Ostrander paused. "But I say to you, temperance *is* our business! Women and innocent children are the ones who suffer when demon rum takes hold."

"Amen! Amen!" several voices called.

Caroline noticed many ladies nodding their heads in approval.

"I say to you all, the call now is 'Woman, be up and doing!'" Mrs. Ostrander rapped her knuckles against the hard wood lectern. "Let your voice be heard!"

There were two more speakers, but none were as engaging as Mrs. Ostrander. Caroline kept thinking about her words as the meeting came to an end.

"Temperance has become a women's cause," Aunt Jane said on the way home. "As you could see for yourself, the meeting was made up mostly of ladies. Though of course, Uncle Elisha does his part." She reached out and patted Uncle Elisha's arm.

"Well, I do what I can, but I think the ladies can achieve a great deal on their own," Uncle Elisha said. "The female population is a force to be reckoned with, and I do believe we should give the ladies the vote."

Caroline glanced sideways at Uncle Elisha. He certainly did have very forward-thinking views. She found herself wondering if her father would have thought the same way if he were still alive.

"Oh, dear brother, if only more men thought like you." Aunt Margaret sighed. Then she cocked her head, looking thoughtful.

"Up and doing. I like that notion of Mrs. Ostrander's. I plan to always be up and doing. How about you, young lady?" She glanced at Caroline, smiling.

Caroline nodded. "Up and doing. I like it too."

Sunday Outing

On Sunday morning, Caroline put on her blue serge and went back to church with her family. She saw many of the same ladies sitting in the pews. Reverend Whitley gave the sermon, though this time he spoke about the need to do unto others as you would have them do unto you, rather than about demon rum.

After church, Uncle Elisha winked at Caroline as he helped her into the buggy. "Now prepare yourself, my dear. You're in for quite a spectacle—the Sunday parade!"

Caroline had no idea what Uncle Elisha meant. At home Mother made them sit inside and read the Bible after church. There were certainly no parades on the Sabbath.

Uncle Elisha flicked the reins, and the horse went trotting toward the center of town. The streets were not very crowded, and all the shops were shuttered tight since it was Sunday. The sky overhead was a perfect blue with puffy white clouds floating over the tops of the buildings.

After they had passed over the Spring Street bridge, Uncle Elisha said, "Get ready for the show!" and Caroline saw that the wide boulevard was crowded with all manner of fine carriages and buggies and horses and riders.

It was not really a parade like on the Fourth of July, Caroline realized. Folks were out taking Sunday drives, just as some did in Concord. But here there were many more people. Caroline sat a little taller in her seat. All at once there was so much to see, she didn't want to miss a single moment.

"Do not worry," Uncle Elisha said dryly. "It

will take us quite a while to reach the end of this adventure." He gestured ahead, indicating how slowly the carriages in front of them were moving.

There were two lines of buggies, one going up the street and one going down it. Everyone was dressed in their Sunday best. Men wore frock coats and tall black hats. Ladies wore fine dresses of silk and satin and lace, with matching bonnets and parasols to shield themselves from the sun.

The street was crowded, and so were the sidewalks on either side. Couples strolled arm in arm and large families walked together, the older children trying to keep the younger ones in line.

Caroline thought of Martha and Eliza. How they would love to see all the beautiful ladies and handsome gentlemen! She looked about, trying to take everything in, so she could describe this scene later in a letter to her family.

"I suppose our Young Man About Town is right," Uncle Elisha said. "Sidesaddle does seem to be quite popular with the ladies."

"Yes. One used to hardly ever see ladies

riding just for fun," Aunt Jane commented.

Caroline watched as a small group of horses and riders went trotting by. Two of the riders were ladies, dressed in stylish velvet riding costumes. One of them smiled and nodded to Caroline as she passed.

At the end of the street, there was a little roundabout, and everyone made the turn and went right back down the same street. Upon Aunt Jane's urging, Uncle Elisha made one round. Then he growled in mock anger, "Enough is enough! I am getting hungry."

Caroline thought they would head home, but Aunt Jane had planned a whole Sunday outing. They were going to meet Alice and William and Billy at the Milwaukee Gardens for a picnic lunch.

"Mr. Bach's orchestra is playing, so it will be quite a treat," Aunt Jane said.

Again Caroline felt surprised. She did not think Mother would approve of listening to a band on Sunday, unless the band played hymns. She wondered what kind of music Mr. Bach's orchestra played. In any case, she told herself that Aunt Jane and Uncle Elisha were responsible for her while she was in Milwaukee, and she could hardly say no to their plans without being rude. She felt disloyal to her mother, but deep down she couldn't help but also feel a little excited.

Uncle Elisha turned down Fourteenth Street, and soon they were driving beside a green rolling meadow surrounded by a white picket fence. The meadow itself was dotted with small shade trees and rosebushes.

Uncle Elisha parked the buggy under a long open shed with other carriages. Then they joined all the other Sunday strollers on a cobblestone path that meandered over the lawn amidst trees and flowers.

"This park is fairly new," Uncle Elisha explained to Caroline as they walked. "It's like having a bit of the country right here in the bustling city. Peaceful and quiet."

Uncle Elisha's words made Caroline think about how peaceful and quiet it was at home. It was strange in a way that city folks wanted a bit of the country in their midst.

"Hallo there!" a voice called behind them.

Caroline turned to see William and Alice. William was carrying a large picnic basket and a blanket. Beside him another you man carried Billy high upon his shoulders. The young man looked a good deal like Uncle Elisha.

Caroline knew this must be Johnny. She had heard her cousin from her bedroom, coming home late at night and leaving early in the morning, but she had not yet seen him.

"And where did you find this stranger?" Uncle Elisha asked teasingly.

"He knew Alice was preparing a feast and came running," William joked.

"Well, Johnny, my boy, come say hello to your cousin," Uncle Elisha ordered.

"Howdee do, Cousin Caroline!" Johnny said. "Welcome to Milwaukee."

Something about his grin and the mischievous look in the eye reminded Caroline of her brother Henry, and she felt instantly at ease with him.

"Hello, Johnny," she replied.

Billy tugged on Johnny's hair, standing it on end, and Johnny began to prance around in a circle like a horse.

"We were just on our way to the carousel," Johnny called. "Would you like to come, Caroline?"

"Oh, yes," Caroline answered. She had read about carousels in *Godey's*, but she had never seen one. Again she felt a little guilty, thinking of Mother, but Uncle Elisha said, "Let's all go!" and she followed as the family strolled across the lawn and down a little hill.

After a moment, Caroline heard the soft sound of music, and up ahead she saw a round structure with a yellow pointed roof and bright red poles. Inside, colorful horses, giant birds, fanged tigers, and other creatures went around and around.

Soon the carousel began to slow. Billy looked down at Caroline from atop Johnny's shoulders and said, "You ride too!"

Caroline wanted very much to ride, but she wondered what Mother would say. She also wondered how much it cost.

"Go on," Uncle Elisha urged, taking a penny from his pocket and handing it to the carousel man.

"We'll ride together!" Alice tucked Caroline's arm under hers.

"Thank you, Uncle," Caroline called back as Alice led her toward two giant swans.

"Let's sit here," Alice said, patting a bench that ran between the swans. She waved to Billy as Johnny helped him up onto a wooden horse. In a moment the music began again and the carousel started up.

Round and round they went. The blue sky and the green grass and the colors of the ladies and gentlemen surrounding the carousel all blurred together. Alice let out a merry laugh and Caroline joined her. She could not stop smiling. She wanted to keep riding the carousel, it was so much fun, but after a while the whirling began to slow, and then the carousel stopped completely.

"Again, again!" Billy yelled, but William told him they were going to the menagerie now, and that satisfied him.

The menagerie was like a long skinny barn, with stalls on each side. Inside the stalls were all kinds of live animals: a pony and a cow and some sheep and goats and pigs. There was also a spotted fawn and a small black bear.

Billy loved the bear best of all, but Caroline thought he looked rather sad in his pen with a large collar and chain around his neck.

"There are bears where Caroline lives," William told his son, and Billy looked at Caroline with big saucer eyes.

Johnny knelt down beside Billy. "When we were little boys, your father and I went to visit Caroline's family. We went out exploring, and we saw a great black bear and her cubs."

"Have you seen bears?" Billy asked Caroline.

"Oh yes," Caroline said. "We have to keep the meat in the trees and the chickens in the coop and everything locked up in the barn. Otherwise the bears might come and eat up our supplies."

Billy took Caroline's hand as they walked. He kept looking up at Caroline as if she herself might turn into a bear.

As they left the menagerie, Uncle Elisha took out his pocket watch and announced it was nearly time for the orchestra to play. They hurried across the lawn and through a grove of trees. Groups of picnickers had already gathered near a raised platform. Uncle Elisha found a shady spot and Caroline helped spread out the quilt and unpack the picnic basket.

Alice had brought little round balls of minced beef and cabbage rolls stuffed with pork and rice. She had also brought smoked herring to eat with thick slices of bread and boiled eggs and cucumber pickles. For a special treat she had made small round white cakes with a lingonberry sauce drizzled on top.

Caroline's mouth watered as she gazed at the good food. "It looks delicious," she told Alice.

"Old family recipes," Alice replied. "I hope you enjoy it all."

"I'm sure I will," Caroline said, but before she could fill a plate, a ripple of applause made her look up.

A group of men wearing black suits and gold-trimmed caps was stepping onto the platform. Each man carried a brass instrument except for the conductor, who carried a long baton. The conductor bowed to the audience, then turned and signaled to the band.

There was a moment of deep silence before the air crashed with music. Several children, including Billy, jumped up and clapped and danced. The orchestra was playing a lively march, not a church hymn, and Caroline's thoughts returned again to Mother and home. She could picture her family sitting quietly in the parlor while Mother read aloud from the Bible. She wondered what Mother would say if she could see her at this very moment.

Caroline glanced about at her aunt and uncle and cousins. They all seemed joyous and content. Obviously they saw nothing wrong with spending their Sunday this way.

"Are you enjoying yourself?" Aunt Jane asked, turning to Caroline, a look of concern in her eyes.

"Yes, thank you," Caroline quickly replied. She did not want to insult her aunt and uncle. She also realized it was true. She *was* enjoying herself. She was glad to be with her Milwaukee family, listening to such happy music on a glorious, sun-filled day.

To College

Caroline awoke bright and early the next day, long before there were any voices rising up from the street below. In the soft morning light she stood at the mirror trying to decide how to fix her long brown hair.

First she braided it and tried to work the braids into a twist like the one she had noticed on a few ladies at the Sunday parade. But she couldn't make it look the way she wanted it to. So she combed her hair out long again and wound it into a simple knot at the nape of her neck. But that seemed too ordinary.

She tried one style and then another, but nothing seemed right and her fingers felt clumsy. She was nearly in tears when Nora came bustling into the room with a pitcher of water.

"There now, miss, let me help you," Nora said in a soft voice. She took the brush from Caroline's hand and led her to a chair. "I do miss fixing my sister's hair like I did when we were wee things."

As Nora's firm fingers worked through her hair, Caroline closed her eyes and felt herself relaxing a little. She remembered how Grandma used to braid her hair before school when she was a little girl, and how it had always made her feel better when she was upset. She felt better now, and when she opened her eyes and looked in the mirror, she exclaimed, "Oh, Nora thank you!"

Nora had parted her hair in the middle and looped it back and twisted it into a French knot. The style was simple but elegant, and it made Caroline feel pretty and sophisticated.

"Yes, I think that will do," Nora said, standing back to admire her handiwork. "Now hurry down to breakfast, miss. I've made some nice fresh rolls this morning."

Caroline washed her face, put on her blue serge, and buttoned up her casaque jacket. Then she took up her satchel and stood in front of the mirror for a last look. She was pleased with what she saw.

"You are going to college, Caroline Lake Quiner," she whispered to her own reflection. The words sounded so unreal when she spoke them out loud, Caroline felt that she should pinch herself to wake up. But she was awake, and she was going to be late if she did not hurry.

Downstairs her aunt and uncle were already at the table.

"Eat up! Eat up!" Uncle Elisha cried, rubbing his hands together. "Must have strength for your first day!"

Even though Nora's rolls were light and flaky, Caroline could make herself swallow only a few small bites. Her stomach was too fluttery.

"Oh, what about a dinner pail?" she blurted, suddenly wondering what she would do at noon. Back home she had always taken a dinner pail and eaten at school, but perhaps she would be expected to go home for dinner here in the city.

"A dinner pail?" Aunt Jane looked perplexed, then her brow smoothed. "Ah, yes, there is a dining hall at the school, my dear. The dinner is part of the tuition."

"Oh," Caroline said, thinking about how very costly the school must be if the tuition included dinner.

"We'd best be off now," Uncle Elisha said, checking his pocket watch. "I'll pull the buggy round front."

"Yes, sir," Caroline replied, hurrying to put on her bonnet and gather up her satchel. She was surprised that her uncle was taking time away from the newspaper on a Monday to drive her, but he had said that he had to be in that part of the city to interview a ship captain about the harbor.

Aunt Jane gave her a hug. "I know you will

do well on your first day," she said encouragingly.

Caroline could only nod and smile. Everything was a blur as she got into the buggy and it rolled away from the house.

Uncle Elisha began to tell her about the new harbor and how it would be safer for ships, but Caroline's mind was too scattered to listen properly.

She opened and closed the clasp on her satchel, checking and rechecking the things inside. She smoothed the skirt of her dress and worried with the ribbons on her bonnet. She was just wondering if she should have polished her shoes again when she felt the buggy come to a halt.

"Here we are," Uncle Elisha said.

Caroline looked up and felt all courage draining out of her. "Is this . . . is this really the school?" she whispered.

"Indeed it is," Uncle Elisha replied. "Miss Beecher chose the design herself when she moved the school to a new building. It is in the gothic style of architecture."

Caroline did not know anything about architecture. All she knew was that the enormous structure in front of her seemed more like a castle out of a storybook than any school she had ever known.

The building was two stories high and took up the whole block. It was made of dark, shiny stone, and it had arching stained-glass windows and spires rising straight up to the sky.

On the stairs leading up to the huge mahogany doors, groups of girls in stylish dresses stood chatting with one another. Caroline knew she must join those girls, but she sat still, feeling a cold rush of fear.

"You know, Caroline, everybody gets a bit shaky on the first day of school." Uncle Elisha's voice was gentle. "Why, I remember how your father used to be scared silly when we boys had to go back to school for the winter. Used to say he'd sooner face a wilderness full of wild animals than a room full of strangers and one new teacher every term."

It sounded so much like something her brother Henry would say, Caroline found herself smiling. She thought of how tall and strong her father had seemed when she was young. It was strange to think of him as a boy afraid of school.

Caroline leaned up and gave her uncle a kiss on the cheek. "Thank you," she said softly.

Uncle Elisha seemed surprised and pleased by the kiss. He grinned and helped her to the ground and wished her well.

Caroline turned and surveyed the colorful scene. Then she took a deep breath and made herself put one foot in front of the other.

Once she was up the stone steps and through the great doors, it felt like she had entered a church. The loud outside voices lowered to a reverential murmur. The light streaming through the stained-glass windows gave the immense entry hall a soft glow, and wood floors gleamed. The ceiling arched high overhead, and great brass lamps hung from the rafters.

Caroline looked around uncertainly. Then she saw that a desk was set up along one wall. She stood in a line of girls all waiting to speak with two prim, gray-haired ladies with ledgers open before them.

"Name please?" one of the ladies asked when it was Caroline's turn. "Quiner . . . Quiner . . . let us see . . ." She ran her finger down a list of names. "Ah, here we are. Caroline Quiner. Room four with Miss Howe." She pointed with her quill pen. "Just down that hallway. Last room on the left."

Caroline was about to head in that direction when the lady stopped her.

"First there is an assembly, Miss Quiner. The principal will address the entire school."

The assembly hall was just off the main room. Caroline made her way down the center aisle, looking for an empty chair in the nearly full rows. She passed girls in groups chatting. Some of the girls stopped to glance at Caroline and smile. Others did not smile but looked Caroline up and down.

Caroline felt the color rising in her cheeks, but she made her eyes stay straight ahead and she kept her chin up. She thought of how Martha had said that city girls would be snooty and that Caroline might feel out of place. But she also remembered how Mother had always said she had taught her daughters to know how to behave in any situation.

Caroline found a seat and waited for the assembly to begin. She listened to the sound of rustling skirts and chatting voices. In a little while, there was a hush. The lady who had helped Caroline at the registration desk appeared at a podium set up at the front of the room.

"Good morning, young ladies. It gives me great pleasure to introduce our principal, Miss Mary Mortimer."

There was applause as the principal walked crisply down the aisle, her stiff petticoats rustling. She was a petite lady, with brown hair pulled neatly back in a chignon. When she spoke, her voice carried into every corner of the room.

"I would like to take this opportunity to welcome you all to Milwaukee Female College. Here at the college we are dedicated to providing an elevated and invigorating course of mental and moral discipline for young ladies."

Miss Mortimer paused, and her large brown eyes swept the room.

"It is our belief, and the belief of our esteemed founder, Miss Catharine Beecher, that young ladies should be thoroughly educated for the arduous duties that await them in their future lives.

"Some of you may assume your domestic duties right away. Others may assume the duties of schoolteacher. Whatever path is set before you, your duties will demand a quickness of perception and a steadiness of purpose. And that is what we intend to cultivate in you here at the college. "

Miss Mortimer paused once more. Caroline felt all the young ladies sitting up a little taller in their seats at Miss Mortimer's speech.

Miss Mortimer cleared her throat and continued. "I have no doubt that some of you may find the work challenging at times. I have no doubt that some of you may in fact feel that you are failing at times. But I leave you with these words, scholars: Endeavor always to do your best, give your best, and I am certain that you will always succeed."

The room filled with applause, and the assembly was over. Caroline stood and followed all the other girls filing out through the doors. As she walked down the hallway, she caught sight of sunny classrooms and clean desks and she felt her heart singing. She wished Mother could be here to see how wonderfully clean and proper everything was.

Miss Howe was standing at the door to Room 4, greeting everyone. She smiled warmly at each girl who passed.

"Welcome to my classroom, scholars. You will find a place for your things in the back. Seating is arranged alphabetically. Please look for your name cards on the desks. You have a few moments before class begins."

Quickly Caroline found a place to hang her jacket and bonnet, then turned to look for her seat. It was near the back not far from the windows. She thought this was a good sign, since that was always her favorite place back home.

Three girls were standing beside her desk already, whispering. They watched Caroline as she set down her satchel.

"You must be Caroline Quiner," one of the girls said. She had a round, pink face framed by blond spaniel curls. When Caroline nodded, she continued in a quick breathless way. "Well, I am Millie—Millie Roberts, and we had better like one another, for we are sharing this seat!" Her sentence ended in a soft peal of giggles.

The girl standing beside Millie glanced at Caroline's dress and said, "That is a fetching design. Did Mrs. Samms make it for you, by chance?"

"N-n-no," Caroline stammered, glancing down and nervously smoothing her skirt with one hand.

"Well, it is charming enough to be one of hers," the girl continued. She was slender and very pretty, with shining black hair and dark, almond-shaped eyes. "Mama won't let anyone but Mrs. Samms make our clothes." She smoothed down the flounces of her light green silk dress.

There was a moment of silence, and then

the third girl, who had red hair and green eyes, leaned around the other two. "I am Louvina Jamison. And this vain creature is Zilpha Maddox."

"I am not vain! What a mean thing to say!" Zilpha cried, pouting.

Louvina laughed, and then she said to Caroline, "Don't mind us. We have been friends for ages."

"But it's fun to meet someone new," Millie quickly added, giggling again.

Just then Miss Howe rang a little handbell and said, "Please find your seats, young ladies."

Everyone hurried to her desk. Caroline and Millie glanced at each other, and Millie smiled and giggled softly. Caroline smiled back. She felt relieved. At least her neighbor seemed friendly.

"Good morning, class," Miss Howe said.

"Good morning, Miss Howe," all the girls responded.

Miss Howe began by explaining the daily schedule.

"Your mornings will be spent in intellectual exercise. Your afternoons will be spent in domestic study and calisthenic exercises. At the end of the day, you will return to this classroom for a quiet study session to review your lessons before you return home."

Miss Howe paused.

"Are there any questions?"

Caroline wondered what calisthenic exercises were, but she was not brave enough to raise her hand.

"Very well. We shall begin with English grammar, composition, and a study of classic literature. After a brief recess, Miss Compton will engage you in the study of mathematics. After that, Miss Towbridge will conduct a course of geography and history."

In her whole life Caroline had never had more than one teacher at a time. In the one-room schoolhouses she had always attended, there was only one teacher, who taught every subject. Now she would have several different teachers. Caroline hoped they were all as nice as Miss Howe seemed.

"Since this is our first day of classes, let us begin with poetry," Miss Howe said, her eyes sparkling.

She asked the girls in the front row to pass out books, and for an hour they read several poems by William Wordsworth and then worked on grammar and spelling. At the end of the second hour, Miss Howe had them put away their books.

"I would like you to write a quick composition on what you hope to achieve here at the college."

Caroline took up her pen and thought for a moment, and then she began to write about how she hoped to become a schoolteacher.

"Oh, you wrote so much!" Millie whispered to Caroline when at last she put down her pen. "I could hardly think of a thing to say!"

"I like to write," Caroline said simply.

Miss Howe brought them to attention and collected the compositions.

"Alas, my time with you has come to an end for now," she said, gathering up her things on the desk. "Please feel free to stand up and move about the room for the few minutes before Miss Compton arrives." She paused at the door. "Circulation! Very important to keep the blood flowing to the brain."

With that, Miss Howe left the room. At first no one moved, but then a few girls stood and walked to the windows to look out. Millie glanced at Caroline and giggled, and they both stood up and moved toward the windows too.

Caroline had not realized how close the school was to the lake. She could see the great masts of the ships and the blue water shimmering in the sun.

"Those are my papa's ships just over there," Millie said, pointing to a group of schooners docked together. "He is in the shipping business."

"My uncle is writing a story on the new harbor in his newspaper," Caroline said.

"Papa is very excited about the new harbor," Millie replied. "He believes it will make us one of the best ports in America."

"So your uncle works for a newspaper, Caroline?" Zilpha asked. She and Louvina had come up beside them.

"He owns the *Milwaukee Weekly Register*," Caroline answered, feeling proud as she said it.

"I think Papa takes that newspaper," Millie said.

"Do you live with your uncle then?" Zilpha persisted.

Caroline told them a little about her family and how she had come to Milwaukee to go to school.

"You must be quite the scholar to come to study here from the country," Zilpha said.

"Of course she is." Millie jumped in before Caroline could think of what to reply. "Why, I saw how much she wrote on her composition. I could hardly think of a word to put down." She giggled. "And I am quite simply terrified of mathematics. But Papa said it would be good for me."

"I don't like mathematics either." Caroline spoke up, and Millie gave her a warm smile.

In a few minutes, Miss Compton came through the door and bade the scholars to return to their seats. She was not as young or energetic as Miss Howe, but her face lit up as she spoke about her subject.

"Mathematics induces habits of investigation and correct reasoning," she told the class.

Caroline decided that this was an interesting way to look at a subject she had never liked. For an hour she diligently worked at the problems Miss Compton wrote on the blackboard.

After mathematics, there was another short recess, and then Miss Towbridge entered the room.

"Think, think, think, young ladies!" she cried, rapping a ruler on the desk and making several scholars jump. "There are many in polite society who do not believe ladies are able to think for themselves. But here at the college, we would like to encourage you to use the good sense God gave you."

Caroline wanted to think, think, think, but she was beginning to feel a little overwhelmed. As she tried to take notes on Miss Towbridge's history lesson, she remembered how Henry had once said that too much learning made him dizzy. Caroline had thought her brother was just being lazy, but now she knew what he meant. She was glad when Miss Towbridge closed her book and dismissed the class for dinner recess so that she could rest her brain for a little while.

Peculiar Notions

Inside the vast dining hall, long wooden tables and benches were set up in neat rows. All classes were supposed to sit and dine together. The teachers ate at their own table near the front of the room.

The food was already on the table when Caroline took her seat beside Millie. It was a simple meal of roast chicken and boiled potatoes and thick, crusty bread, but everything tasted delicious to Caroline. Since she hadn't eaten much breakfast, she ate everything on her plate. Millie picked at her food.

"Mama says I must lose several inches around my waist." Millie sighed. "She is hoping that Miss Beecher's calisthenics will help."

"They say that Miss Mortimer had a terrible limp before she began a series of calisthenics," Zilpha whispered.

"A limp, you say?" Louvina asked. "Why, she didn't appear to limp at all."

"No, she didn't," Millie said.

Finally Caroline had to ask. "What are calisthenics?"

"You don't know about Miss Beecher's calisthenics?" Zilpha asked, her eyes wide with surprise.

"Well, you are in for a surprise then!" Louvina cried.

"We have to prance about in our shifts!" Zilpha told her. "And the teacher throws open the windows, even in the coldest weather. Last year my cousin Lydia caught a dreadful chill that lasted weeks and weeks, and so Mother almost did not enroll me, but Father insisted that I would benefit from Miss Beecher's peculiar notions."

"Peculiar notions?" Caroline asked.

"Oh, the calisthenics," Zilpha said, waving a hand in the air.

"Miss Beecher has peculiar notions about dress as well," Louvina said.

"She doesn't believe in corsets," Millie whispered.

"Well, she does not believe in tight stays," Zilpha corrected. "In any case, you won't be wearing your corsets during calisthenics, let me assure you, girls!"

Millie looked flustered. "Mama says a lady must always wear her corset. I wear it day and night, don't you?"

Zilpha shook her head. "I myself would be happy to be free as a bird."

"Well, you don't need one," Millie replied, eyeing Zilpha's tiny waist.

Caroline was not sure what to think. Mother said a young lady must always wear corsets, though she did not approve of keeping them very tight, especially during chores.

"I doubt Miss Beecher would approve of hoops," Zilpha continued. "But mark my words, I will have them for the winter season."

"Oooh!" Louvina squealed. "I do so want one!"

"Mrs. Samms says they are light as air," Zilpha said.

Caroline remembered seeing an advertisement for hoops in the *Register.* Now she wanted to ask what they were, but at the same time she didn't want Zilpha to look at her again as if she were just a country girl. The talk between the girls was so quick that Caroline felt a little slow next to them.

When dinner recess was over, the girls were all expected to help clear the tables.

"You see, more of Miss Beecher's peculiar notions," Zilpha whispered. "In other schools, the young ladies are waited upon."

Caroline couldn't help but smile a little at Zilpha's comment. How different she was from these girls! Until she had come to Milwaukee, she had never in her life been waited upon. She did not think doing a simple chore like clearing the dishes was peculiar at all.

The domestic arts class was held in a room that had been outfitted just like a kitchen. There were rows of cookstoves, worktables, and basins. Neat shelves were lined with all manner of pots and pans and bowls and cookware.

"Here you will learn the basics of how to run a household properly and efficiently," the teacher, Miss Hotchkiss, informed them.

They were each given two books. One was *A Treatise for Domestic Economy, for the Use of Young Ladies at Home and at School.* The other was a book of recipes. Both had been written by Miss Beecher.

"Keep these volumes at hand always, girls," Miss Hotchkiss implored. "You will never go wrong if you follow Miss Beecher's advice."

Caroline quickly glanced through the recipes for medicines and poultices, vegetable and meat dishes, and hearty soups. She thought how Mother kept all these things inside her head. It was convenient that someone like Miss Beecher had actually taken the time to write it all down and publish a book.

"Before beginning the cooking class, we will begin with an overview of the principles of health so that you will better understand the effects of nourishment on the human system," Miss Hotchkiss said.

Miss Hotchkiss had them turn to the opening pages of Miss Beecher's *Treatise*, and for an hour she took them through the workings of the human body. In the book there were engravings of a human skeleton. Several young ladies looked as if they were going to faint, but Miss Hotchkiss chided them.

"How will you be able to nurse the sick if you are called upon to do so if you do not understand some basic principles of the human form?" Miss Hotchkiss asked.

One of the bolder girls replied, "Mother always calls for the doctor."

"Where possible a doctor should be called, by all means," Miss Hotchkiss replied. "But you may find yourself ministering to the sick without benefit of a doctor. A woman need not have the minute and extensive knowledge of a physician, but she should gain a general knowledge of the first principles, as a guide to her judgment in emergencies when she can rely on no other aid."

With that, Miss Hotchkiss told them to close their books and come forward to put on aprons and caps. Now they would begin their cooking lessons.

"We will begin with something simple," Miss Hotchkiss said. "There is a growing fashion to serve fancy meals. But let me assure you that good food need not be dressed up. Here we will learn to prepare nourishing and stimulating food."

Miss Hotchkiss broke the class into little groups, and they began with a lesson on breadmaking.

"Bread is the staff of life, after all," Miss Hotchkiss said.

Caroline had been making bread since she was a little girl, and so she found the lesson an easy one. Millie seemed at ease as well, but Zilpha and Louvina both were awkward. Caroline realized that they probably had cooks and maids like Nora.

At the end of the class, all the girls hung up their aprons and caps and headed for calisthenics class.

"I am glad I am wearing a new shift," Millie whispered to Caroline.

Caroline was glad all her underthings were new as well, but as it turned out, Zilpha had been misinformed. When they came to the calisthenics hall, they were given special calisthenics costumes to wear over their shifts.

"Please remove your dresses and corsets and attire yourselves in these costumes, which Miss Beecher designed herself," the teacher, Miss LaRue, instructed.

"Well, it's almost like wearing nothing but your shift anyway," Zilpha whispered.

The costumes were loose-fitting blouses and skirts made of light muslin.

Caroline's stomach did a quick somersault at the thought of changing her clothes in front of strangers, but when she followed the others into the changing room, she saw that long curtains had been arranged in such a way as to give each girl privacy.

"Remove your stockings and your shoes as well, girls!" Miss LaRue called through the curtains.

There were squeals of dismay and a few giggles, but all the girls submitted to Miss LaRue's commands. Caroline was used to going barefoot during the summer months, even to school. But she knew city girls probably did not go barefoot.

When Caroline came out of the changing room, she felt very self-conscious. But she had to admit that with the sun streaming through the open windows, and the breeze blowing the muslin skirts, all the girls looked very pretty.

Miss LaRue had all the girls line up along one wall. "Before we begin, I will become acquainted with your spines and how each of you carries herself."

Miss LaRue made her way down the line, placing her hands on girls' shoulders and drumming her fingers down the spine.

When she came to Caroline, she said approvingly, "A lovely spine, my dear. A lovely spine. Let's try to keep it that way."

To Millie she said, "We will need to work on your posture, young lady. I can see you have a tendency to hunch your shoulders."

Millie blushed as Miss LaRue moved on to the next girl, and Caroline gave her a reassuring smile.

After all the girls had been looked over and pronouncements had been made, Miss LaRue clapped her hands and turned to speak to the lady at the pianoforte.

"Now, Miss Fleming, please play us something lively."

Miss Fleming lifted her hands above the keyboard and brought them lightly down. A quick, lively melody echoed through the room.

"Miss Beecher in her wisdom has devised an ingenious series of graceful movements beneficial to the human frame," Miss LaRue explained. "Today we will begin with a simple repetition, and each day we will add to it, so that in a few weeks' time, you will be able to do the entire series with ease."

With that she began to demonstrate Miss Beecher's calisthenics. She raised her hands high over her head, and then she bent forward until her fingers nearly touched the ground. She repeated this energetically several times, and then told the girls to follow her movements.

There was more giggling as the girls glanced at one another and raised their arms over their heads. Caroline felt like giggling too, but she made herself keep quiet. She lifted her arms high and then slowly let herself bend at the waist. Her fingertips almost touched her toes.

"Up, down! Up, down!" Miss LaRue instructed.

Caroline began to feel a little breathless. Warmth flooded through her, and she knew her cheeks must be pink and flushed. She had a sudden image of Henry's smirking face. She knew how silly she must look.

"Good!" Miss LaRue cried. "Now let us hold our arms out like this." She stretched her arms out wide so that they were parallel to the floor. Then she began to twist her trunk to and fro so that her arms made a circular motion. "Your arms are the branches of a young sapling. Supple but strong."

Caroline closed her eyes. As she moved her arms as Miss LaRue instructed, she pictured the trees surrounding her home, branches moving in a gentle breeze.

"Now we will march!" Miss LaRue announced.

First the girls marched in place; then Miss LaRue had them march in widening circles about the room, their arms swinging in time to the lively music from Miss Fleming's piano. Caroline remembered marching as a little girl at Fourth of July celebrations. It seemed strange to be marching now that she was a young lady, but she had to admit it was invigorating. She no longer felt dizzy and tired, as she had in Miss Towbridge's class. Her head felt perfectly clear.

"I advise each of you to take a daily round of exercises in addition to these calisthenics!" Miss LaRue called above the music and marching feet. "Walking, strolling. These will do wonders for your heart and soul, not to mention your figures and your complexions."

Finally Miss LaRue had them stop near the open window. She took a deep breath and exhaled loudly. "We will keep the windows open in good weather and in bad," she announced. "Ventilation. Circulation. Highly important. Good clean air, and lots of it." She went down the line of girls, encouraging them all to breath deeply. Then she dismissed class for the day.

There was a great deal of giggling and whispering as the girls hurried to change back into their dresses.

"Well, what did you think?" Millie asked Caroline once they were heading downstairs to their final class of the day.

"It was peculiar," Caroline said slowly, and then she felt herself smiling. "But I must admit it was fun."

"I thought so too!" Zilpha cried. "And I would like to see if what Miss LaRue said is true. About exercise benefiting one's figure and complexion." She glanced around the little group, her dark eyes sparkling merrily. "I propose that we meet in the morning and walk to school. How does that sound?"

"Yes! Let's do!" Millie and Louvina cried together. Then Millie turned to Caroline. "Oh, and where is your uncle's home, Caroline?" she asked.

For a moment Caroline forgot the names of the streets, but then she remembered.

"The corner of Cass and Lyon?" Zilpha repeated. "That's not very far from us. Let us meet on the corner of Jefferson and Division at seven thirty, then."

"I will have to ask my aunt and uncle," Caroline said. She wondered for a brief moment if it was really safe to walk all the way to school, but she knew it must be because Zilpha had suggested it.

"Of course they will let you!" Zilpha scoffed.

Caroline quickly glanced at Zilpha. From her tone, she guessed that Zilpha was accustomed to getting her way.

Back in Room 4, Miss Howe announced that the final hour would be spent in quiet study. Caroline opened the textbook Miss Towbridge had distributed and read through the assignments for the next day, but she found it difficult to concentrate. Her mind swirled with all she had done that day. When Miss Howe dismissed class, all the girls hurried to the back to collect their jackets and bonnets and then streamed out into the late-afternoon air.

"I hope to see you tomorrow morning," Millie called to Caroline as she waved goodbye.

Caroline stood uncertainly on the steps for a moment, glancing about, and then she saw Aunt Jane in the buggy waving at her.

"So?" Aunt Jane asked as Caroline climbed in. "How was your first day?"

"It was wonderful," Caroline answered, "but did you know about Miss Beecher's peculiar notions?"

"Peculiar notions? Whatever do you mean, my dear?"

"Well, we have to do calisthenic exercises," Caroline said.

"Oh, yes, calisthenics are all the rage back east. Exercise is very important, I believe.

That is why I take my walks to the lake."

Caroline felt relieved to know that her aunt approved. But she did not think she would write home about the calisthenics. She thought about how Henry would laugh out loud. And she didn't want Mother to think she had spent all her money on sending Caroline to college to prance around a room.

The New Fashion

The next morning Caroline stood anxiously at the corner of Jefferson and Division Streets. Aunt Jane and Uncle Elisha had given their permission to walk with her new friends, and Caroline wanted to be there early. She wasn't sure she had the courage to walk through the city by herself.

Caroline watched as the streets came to life around her. The lamplighters were turning off the lamps. The hawkers were pushing their carts along, and the merchants were opening their shutters and sweeping the sidewalks in front of their shops.

"Yoo-hoo, Caroline!" a voice called.

Caroline turned to see Millie coming down the street waving a gloved hand in the air. Zilpha and Louvina were with her. The girls made a pretty picture in their bright dresses and with their cheeks flushed from their stroll. For a moment Caroline wondered how she looked in her green wool. But Zilpha immediately commented on it.

"Another lovely frock, Caroline," she said. "You must give me the name of your dressmaker."

Caroline was about to say that her own mother was the seamstress, but something kept her from speaking. It felt good to have Zilpha think she had a fashionable dressmaker to make her clothes.

"I am so glad you could meet us, Caroline," Millie was saying. "Mama thinks this walking will do wonders for my figure. I do feel quite energetic, as Miss LaRue predicted."

They turned, and Millie took Caroline's arm as they began to walk. "I told Papa about you,

Caroline, and he knows of your uncle and his newspaper. And Mama knows your aunt from the Ladies' Aid Society."

Somehow Caroline felt that she was truly being accepted into the group now. The girls asked Caroline about her home in Concord as they strolled.

"Three brothers and three sisters?" Millie cried after Caroline had told them about her family. "Goodness, I can't imagine. I have always wished for a little brother or sister to dote on."

"You can have mine," Louvina said. "My little brother is such a nuisance."

"And what does your family do way out in Concord?" Zilpha asked.

"We have land," Caroline replied. "We grow wheat and corn, and we have a barn with animals."

"Oh! Do you have a horse?" Zilpha asked excitedly. "I do so want a horse of my own to ride."

"No," Caroline replied. "We have two cows and a pair of oxen and some chickens and geese and a pig."

"Well, you should ask your father for a horse," Zilpha said matter-of-factly. "Side-saddle is all the fashion now."

Caroline smiled to herself. She thought of what Pa would say if she asked him for a horse. She also wondered if Zilpha had read her cousin's piece on horseback riding.

"You know, my aunt took my cousins to a farm this summer on an outing," Zilpha was saying. "She said it was quite restful." She turned and looked at Caroline. "Is it restful on your little farm?"

Caroline stifled a laugh. She knew Henry would certainly not think the farm was restful. "It is peaceful," Caroline answered at last. "It is very quiet compared to Milwaukee."

"We must go for a visit someday," Zilpha announced.

"Oh, yes, that would be such fun!" Millie quickly agreed. "We could make a party of it to the country, all three of us! What do you think, Caroline?"

"Yes, that would be nice," Caroline said,

smiling, but deep down she could not really imagine her new friends in the country with their stylish clothes and refined manners. She knew they must be the same age as she was, but they seemed older and more sophisticated, especially when the talk turned to boys.

"Ned Lewiston promised to take me driving in his new buggy on Sunday," Zilpha said. Both Millie and Louvina let out little squeals of delight.

"Oh, I am green with envy," Louvina said. "That Ned Lewiston is quite handsome."

"So is his friend Benjamin Smith," Millie added, giggling.

"Do you have a beau back home, Caroline?" Zilpha asked.

When Caroline shook her head, the girls all looked surprised.

"No one at all? Come now," Millie cried.

"I am going to be a schoolteacher as soon as I can pass my examinations," Caroline explained. "I don't have time for beaus."

"Ah, you are going to 'assume the duties of schoolteacher,'" Zilpha said, mimicking Miss

Mortimer's speech at the assembly. Caroline thought that Zilpha had quite a knack for imitating others.

"Well, you will be a pretty schoolteacher like Miss Howe," Millie said.

"Not an old sourpuss like Miss Towbridge," Zilpha added. She and the other girls giggled, and Caroline couldn't help but giggle a little too.

"Miss Towbridge does have a rather sour disposition and a gray complexion to match," Zilpha declared. "'Tis a wonder she doesn't follow Miss Beecher's advice on the subject of physical exercise."

"She is much too old," Louvina exclaimed. "Can you imagine her in our calisthenics class?"

They all giggled again. Caroline did not want to be cruel, but it was comical to think of Miss Towbridge in a muslin costume, trying to "bend like a young sapling" as Miss LaRue had said.

As the girls walked, the streets became more crowded with the morning rush.

"Oh, look, the hotcake man!" Millie said, pointing down an alleyway where a small crowd had gathered. "Have you gone to the hotcake man yet?" she asked Caroline.

Caroline shook her head, and Millie led her down the alleyway. Right inside an open window a man stood over a hot griddle, making hotcakes. He wore a puffy white hat and a white apron. He poured the thick batter from a china pitcher onto the griddle, then made a great show of flipping the little round cakes.

Caroline's mouth watered as the sweet smell of hotcakes filled the air. She had hardly touched her breakfast again that morning, and now she felt her stomach rumbling. A sign said the hotcakes cost a nickel for two. Caroline had some of the money Mother had given her. She didn't think it would hurt to spend a little of it.

"Oh I do love hotcakes, but I shouldn't have any," Millie fretted.

"Why don't we share them?" Caroline suggested. "I only want one anyway."

"All right then," Millie said, smiling happily.

The golden hotcakes with maple syrup drizzled over them were served on pieces of brown paper. Caroline and Millie shared one order and so did Louvina and Zilpha. The hotcakes were light and fluffy and sweet. Almost as good as Mother made, Caroline thought.

After the hotcakes were eaten, the girls continued on toward school. Zilpha and Louvina and Millie pointed out their favorite shops to Caroline as they walked.

"That is where we all buy our gloves," Zilpha said, pointing to a shop with a hand painted on the plate glass window and the words, "Glove Shoppe—Finest Gloves for Ladies and Gentlemen" stenciled in pretty letters below it.

"And we always buy our bonnets from Mrs. Tibbits." Louvina pointed to another storefront with bonnets displayed in the window.

"Another day we should stop by Mrs. Samms's shop," Zilpha said. "I do believe she has a dress with a hoop on display in her window."

Caroline was so curious, she finally just had

to ask. "What is a hoop?"

"You haven't heard of hoops?" Louvina asked.

"I am surprised your dressmaker doesn't know about them," Zilpha cried. Caroline did not say anything, and Zilpha continued, "Well, they are petticoats, but they are fashioned from thin pieces of steel. They are the new fashion back east. Mother promised I could have one for the Winter Ball."

"I can hardly wait for the Winter Ball," Millie said, sighing. Then she turned to Caroline. "We were all too young to go last year. Perhaps you will be going too?"

"I don't know," Caroline replied. She had no idea if her aunt and uncle attended balls.

When they reached school, Zilpha said they should walk every day.

"Let's make it our daily routine," she proposed.

So every morning and afternoon they walked to and from school together. Caroline came to look forward to the walks just as much as she looked forward to learning new things at school each day. She enjoyed strolling with her new friends, listening to them chatter about the latest fashions. And she enjoyed seeing different parts of the city.

One day the girls decided to walk to school along the lake.

"Over there is where they are making the new harbor," Millie said.

Caroline looked where Millie was pointing. The street simply stopped, and a crew of men were digging, their shovels flashing in the morning light. Caroline remembered what her aunt had said about moving heaven and earth. It looked as if the land were being cut like a piece of cloth.

"It's like the Erie Canal, Father says," Millie said. "Only not so big."

"Look! There's your ship, Millie," Zilpha said, pointing beyond the men to the glittering water where several ships were anchored. Caroline saw that one of the ships had the name *Milwaukee Belle* painted on the side.

"That's my papa's ship, you see," Millie told Caroline. "And that's my name as well.

Milwaukee Belle Roberts."

"What a pretty name," Caroline replied. She had not dreamed that Millie was short for Milwaukee.

"You see, Papa was one of the first settlers here," Millie explained. "He named me after Milwaukee, and then he named the ship after me when I was born."

"What does your ship carry?" Caroline asked as they continued on their way to school.

"Oh, the ships carry all manner of cargo from here back east," Millie said, waving a hand in the air. "Lumber and leather and wheat and brick. Father says all the east is mad for our Milwaukee brick."

"And one day the ship might carry you back east!" Louvina said.

"Yes, perhaps." Millie sighed. "Mama has never been happy here, and Papa has promised to return to New York one day."

"But you won't return before the Winter Ball, that's for certain!" Zilpha said brightly. "Why don't we stop by Mrs. Samms's on the way home today and look at ball dresses?"

"Yes, let's do!" Millie and Louvina said together.

And so after school that day, Caroline got to see her first hooped dress. The dress shop was closed already, but two dresses were on display in the window, with a little card below them that said, "The new fashion."

"Just look!" Millie breathed.

Caroline was quiet as she stood at the window, gazing at the dresses. They were simply the most beautiful dresses she had ever seen. One was a day dress and the other was for evening. Both had skirts that curved like a bell. Caroline knew it would normally take many layers of starched petticoats to achieve the voluminous effect.

"The petticoats are made of steel?" Caroline asked, puzzling over what Zilpha had described.

"Yes, Mrs. Samms showed me," Zilpha said. "They are made of several thin steel hoops, which are all connected by long bands of cotton. It is quite cunning."

The day dress was made of soft blue cotton with wide bell sleeves to match the wide bell shape of the skirt. Tiny seed-pearl buttons ran down the length of the gown, from the tiny scalloped collar to the flounced hemline.

The evening dress was made of yards and yards of pink silk. It had a wide V neckline and short double puffed sleeves. The domed skirt was decorated with several flounces of pink tulle that scalloped into delicate silk roses.

"I must have a dress like that for the Winter Ball, I simply must!" Zilpha whispered.

They stood staring at the dresses and talking about the ball for so long, the lamplighters were already walking up the hill when Caroline got to her uncle's door.

"Goodness!" Aunt Jane said. "I was about to have your uncle go looking for you!"

"Oh, I am sorry, Aunt Jane," Caroline said. "The girls took me by a dress shop." Then she went on to describe the dress.

"Yes, I've seen a few hoops around," Aunt Jane said. "And I've been reading about them for some time. The newspapers your uncle subscribes to back east have had quite a debate about them."

Aunt Jane went next door and asked Aunt Margaret to find the articles and bring them upstairs, and after supper that night Caroline sat in the parlor poring through the eastern newspapers while her aunts knitted and sewed.

Some of the articles were highly amusing. "Every woman today is a tempest," noted one writer. "She cannot enter or leave a room without knocking over everything in her path."

In another article there was an announcement that the New York Omnibus Company had raised fares from seven cents to twelve cents for ladies wearing hoops.

"Ladies in hoops take up more space than is safe or necessary!" they scolded.

But some of the articles made Caroline want to cry. There were reports of ladies not realizing how close their skirts came to fireplaces or to lamps, and catching themselves on fire. There was a terrible story about a lady who had perished after being dragged when the steel hoop caught in her carriage and the horses spooked.

"Oh how awful!" Caroline exclaimed. "Do you really think hoops are dangerous to wear?"

"I'm not sure," Aunt Jane said. "They are rather cumbersome."

Aunt Margaret sighed. "I look forward to the day when women can dress a bit more sensibly without fear of being ridiculed as manly or unfashionable."

Caroline read the newspapers until it was time to go to bed. In the morning she asked Aunt Jane if she might take the newspapers to show her friends.

"By all means," Aunt Jane said.

The girls stopped to read them at a little park on the way to school. "I declare, these writers are silly," Zilpha scoffed.

"The most important thing is that the hoops look good," Louvina said.

"And they are so much lighter than all the petticoats we have to wear to make our skirts look full," Zilpha added.

"I do think the big skirts are very becoming," Millie said hesitantly. She glanced at Caroline and her brow wrinkled. "I suppose one must be careful when wearing them, don't you think?"

"Yes, I do," Caroline replied decidedly.

"These stories don't change my mind," Zilpha said. "I must have a hoop by the winter season, and that's all there is to it!"

Zilpha was not the only one obsessed with hoops. Over the next few days, it seemed that all the girls in the school were talking about hoops. In one class, two girls came to school wearing them, but Miss Mortimer sent the girls home. Then she sent a notice around that hoopskirts were banned from the school because they were impractical for daily wear. Some girls were outraged, but they would not go against the principal.

On Friday, Zilpha met them at the corner, a huge smile on her face.

"I have a surprise!" she said. "Come to tea tomorrow, and you will find out what it is!"

Tea at Zilpha's

On Saturday, Caroline put on her green wool, looked at herself in the mirror, and sighed. She wished she had another dress to wear to tea at Zilpha's. The girls had seen all her outfits by now.

Right away she felt a pang of guilt. She thought of how three good dresses were more than she had ever had in her entire life. Not only that, Mother had used all her savings to make Caroline's new wardrobe.

Caroline was ashamed of her feelings, but she couldn't help it. She was envious of her new friends, especially of Zilpha, who wore a different, beautiful dress every day. She knew Zilpha's family must be wealthy and live in a grand house, and she was right.

As they turned onto Zilpha's street, Uncle Elisha let out a low whistle.

"Pretty fancy address," he said. "I thought I recognized the name Maddox. Her father has made his fortune buying and selling land in these parts. Every day fortunes are being won and lost over land speculation here."

Caroline did not know what her uncle meant, but certainly some kind of fortune had been won. Zilpha's house was a mansion made out of Milwaukee brick, with a square tower in the center and many tall windows glinting in the sun. When Caroline rang the bell, a white-haired maid opened the door.

"Please follow me, miss," the maid said. She led Caroline through an elegant foyer into a parlor twice the size of Aunt Jane's, with shimmering damask curtains and plush carpets on the floor.

Millie and Louvina were already there,

lounging on one of two silken settees. Both girls were wearing dresses Caroline had not seen before. Louvina's was corded silk with wide lacy sleeves, and Millie's was wine-colored wool with black fringe.

"There you are, Caroline," Millie said brightly. "We were just wondering where our hostess could be."

"She is being very mysterious," Louvina added. She stood up and went to the pianoforte. "Do you play, Caroline?"

Caroline shook her head. She sat down beside Millie and listened as Louvina began to play a light, airy tune. Glancing about the room at the rich tapestries and the fine upholstered furnishings, Caroline found herself wondering why Zilpha had been sent to the Milwaukee Female College at all. Surely a girl of Zilpha's standing did not need the kind of practical education the school endorsed. But then again, Uncle Elisha had said that fortunes had been won and lost here. Perhaps her parents were being practical sending Zilpha to college.

"Ah, ladies, it was so good of you to come!" a voice said in mock formality.

Caroline turned to see Zilpha standing at the doorway. She was wearing a day dress just like the one in Mrs. Samms's window. She looked so stylish and sophisticated, Caroline felt a rush of envy. She wondered if the other girls felt it too.

"Oh, Zilpha!" Millie whispered.

"You clever thing," Louvina cried, jumping up from the piano bench.

Zilpha seemed to float as she glided into the room in her wide, sweeping skirt. Her waist was tiny inside the V-shaped bodice, and her dark hair had been curled and fell prettily about her shoulders.

"You look just like a picture from *Godey's*," Caroline breathed, and the others quickly agreed.

"Why, thank you," Zilpha said, smiling and making a little turn to show off her dress. "Girls, I feel as light as a cloud."

She lifted the skirt so they could see what was underneath. The hoop was like a circular cage made out of thin strips of steel. The cage was held together by long pieces of cotton. Caroline couldn't wait to describe this to her mother and sisters. She knew they would be amazed.

"You see, no heavy petticoats at all," Zilpha said.

"What are you wearing underneath?" Louvina demanded.

"They look like drawers!" Millie giggled.

Caroline giggled a little too. It did look like Zilpha was wearing men's drawers, but they had dainty lace trim along the bottom.

"Mrs. Samms calls them 'pantalets,'" Zilpha said.

"Won't you be cold when the weather turns?" Millie asked. "I get tired of dragging around my petticoats, but they do keep me warm."

"Mrs. Samms says she can make the pantalets out of flannel, and you can wear woolens too," Zilpha said. "I don't have to worry about being cold when I'm dancing, though! Mama bought me the ball gown as well. Mrs. Samms is still fitting it. But I can practice dancing in this!"

Zilpha began to hum a lively tune and sway back and forth. The skirt swished prettily with her. In a moment, she caught Millie up to dance with her, but the skirt flipped up on one side, revealing a great deal of Zilpha's leg.

"Oh, my!" Zilpha giggled. "This will take some getting used to." She adjusted her position so that Millie was at arm's length and then began dancing again. "Oh well, a gentleman's arms will be longer than yours, Millie, I daresay."

Louvina went back to the pianoforte and began to play a waltz. Caroline watched the girls dance about the room. Again it appeared as though Zilpha were floating on air. But in a moment, she bumped into a chair and knocked it over. Before she could right the chair, she bumped into a table and sent a book flying.

"Perhaps the newspapers Caroline brought were right. You are a tempest!" Louvina exclaimed, stopping her playing.

Zilpha ignored Louvina and leaned down to

pick up the book from the floor, and her skirt bounced up, revealing nearly her whole backside and her lacy pantalets.

Millie and Louvina almost fell over laughing. Caroline put a hand to her mouth to stifle her laughter. She could tell that Zilpha was not as amused. Her cheeks flushed red, and she looked close to tears.

"We're sorry," Louvina said when she saw Zilpha's expression. "It will just take a little practice is all."

"I suppose so," Zilpha sniffed.

The girls set about helping Zilpha "practice" wearing her hoop. They found that it was necessary for Zilpha to be constantly aware of her surroundings; otherwise she bumped into things. She had to turn sideways in order to fit through doorways. And she had to place a firm hand on her skirt as she ascended or descended the stairs—otherwise the skirt popped up immodestly. Sitting was not particularly easy or comfortable either.

"The bands of steel are soft, but they are not so nice to sit on," Zilpha reported as she nearly fell onto the sofa, looking weary from all the "practicing." Once more the skirt threatened to reveal a good deal of ankle, but Zilpha wrestled it down. "Oh, well," she said, and sighed. "I won't be doing much sitting at the Winter Ball."

"Of course you won't," a voice declared. "When I was your age, I never sat out a single dance."

Caroline turned to see an older version of Zilpha: a beautiful lady with milky white skin and black hair pulled back in a heavy chignon. Caroline guessed this must be Mrs. Maddox.

"Don't slouch, dear," Mrs. Maddox said as she sailed across the room in an elegant silk day dress.

"I was just resting, Mama." Zilpha sighed again, but she sat up straighter, making sure to hold down her skirt.

"Good afternoon, young ladies," Mrs. Maddox greeted Millie and Louvina cordially.

"Good afternoon, Mrs. Maddox," the friends singsonged together.

"And who is this?" Mrs. Maddox turned to Caroline.

"It's Caroline Quiner, Mama," Zilpha said. "Remember, I told you about her?"

"Ah, yes. How nice to meet you." Mrs. Maddox looked Caroline up and down the way the girls at college had done the first day. Caroline found herself glancing quickly down at her own skirt to see if something was spilled there, but of course her dress was as clean as ever.

"How nice to meet you," Caroline said politely. "Thank you for having me in your home."

"A pleasure," Mrs. Maddox answered, but it did not seem as if she meant it. Caroline noticed that Mrs. Maddox's eyes were the same dark brown and lovely almond shape as her daughter's, but they did not sparkle. Even though Mrs. Maddox's lips were smiling, her eyes were not. Caroline felt a chill run through her.

"Have you offered your guests tea?" Mrs. Maddox asked her daughter.

"I was just about to ring for Mary," Zilpha answered. She stood, holding down her skirt, and made her careful way around the settee to tug on a velvet sash near the door. Caroline guessed the sash somehow signaled the maid, because she appeared almost immediately carrying a large silver tray, which she placed on the table in front of the settee. The tray held an ornate silver teapot, dainty china cups and saucers, and a plate of cookies.

"Well, I shall leave you to yourselves again," Mrs. Maddox said. "I only wanted to check in. Enjoy your visit, girls."

"Thank you, Mrs. Maddox," Millie and Louvina said, and Caroline added her thanks as the lady glided out of the room.

Zilpha perched on the settee again, holding down her skirt while the maid poured their tea and then quickly disappeared. The girls gathered on the other settee.

"There's no room next to you," Louvina complained. And it was true. Zilpha took up most of the settee.

Caroline was quiet as the girls chattered

around her. She felt suddenly out of sorts. Mrs. Maddox had seemed haughty, looking at Caroline's dress with disdain. But then again, Caroline might have imagined it. Perhaps Mrs. Maddox was not feeling well.

Caroline tried not think about it, and turned her attention to her friends. Zilpha passed the plate around. Caroline was just about to bite into a cookie when the door opened again and in walked three young men.

"Why, James, what are you doing here?" Zilpha asked, jumping to her feet so quickly that her skirt popped up. Quickly she smoothed it down.

"Sorry to interrupt your tea party, little sister," one of the young men said. Like Zilpha, he was tall and slim, with dark curly hair. "I found these two loafing about the university and decided to take pity on them and invite them home."

"Ned! And Ben! What a pleasant surprise!" Zilpha cried, blushing prettily.

Caroline realized that these were the young men the girls had often discussed on the walks to and from school. Ned was tall, with blond curls and blue eyes, and Ben had sandy brown hair and a wide smile. All three were handsome and well dressed, with creased trousers and jackets and ties. For a moment, Caroline thought of her own brothers and how they hated to get "gussied up," as Henry called it. These young men looked as though they were used to wearing dapper clothes every day of the week, not just Sunday.

"Ah, you are Zilpha's new friend from college," James said once Zilpha had introduced Caroline to the group. "Zilpha says you are quite the scholar."

Caroline glanced quickly into his face, wondering if he would have the same cold expression as his mother. She was surprised by how warm and friendly he seemed. His whole face lit up when he smiled.

"I don't know about being a scholar," Caroline answered, feeling her cheeks turning pink under his gaze.

"Caroline is just being modest," Millie spoke up. "She is much smarter than the rest of us."

Caroline looked down at the cup of tea in her hands. She wasn't sure what to say, and she knew she was blushing.

"Goodness gracious, let's not talk of school today!" Zilpha whirled about. "You boys must tell me what you think of my new dress."

"It is quite fine," Ned responded, his eyes following Zilpha adoringly as she moved carefully about the room to show off her hoop.

"So this is what's all the go back east, then?" James asked, putting a hand to his chin and studying Zilpha's attire. "Not bad, little sister. Not bad."

"I think it is fine!" Ned repeated.

After Zilpha rang for more tea and cookies, she began to chatter with Ned about his new buggy. Louvina and Millie asked after Ben's family. Caroline took small sips of tea and nibbled at the sugary cookie. She wasn't sure what to talk about. She knew a young lady should always be able to make small talk, but she couldn't think of anything to add to the conversations around her. She watched James put a few cookies on his plate. When he straightened up, he caught her eye.

"Your uncle owns the *Milwaukee Weekly Register*, does he not?" James asked.

Caroline dabbed a napkin to her lips to make sure there were no crumbs there before answering. "Why, yes, he does."

"I read your uncle's editorials every week," James said. "I think he has a lot of sense."

"I'll tell my uncle. I'm sure he'll be pleased to know he has an admirer."

"Yes, I do admire his writing," James said enthusiastically. "It must be interesting, the newspaper business." He gave Caroline a questioning look.

"It is!" Caroline found herself exclaiming. "I had no idea before I came here, but it is certainly fascinating to watch the newspaper as it is being printed."

"I wonder, might I be able to visit your uncle's print shop and see for myself sometime?" James asked.

"I'm sure he wouldn't mind," Caroline replied enthusiastically. "The print shop is always busy. Men come in and out all the time to discuss what's going on in the city and the rest of the country."

"And what is going on in the rest of the country?" James asked, looking at her quizzically.

Caroline thought for a moment. "There is much fighting going on in Kansas Territory, or KT, as my uncle calls it, between the Free Staters and the border ruffians who are from Missouri," Caroline replied, choosing her words carefully. "The Missourians are trying to make KT a slave state."

James nodded. "Yes, I've read your uncle's reports on the subject. 'Bloody Kansas,' they're calling it, aren't they?"

Caroline felt a chill run through her. "Yes," she replied solemnly.

"Does your uncle believe that Kansas will become a free state eventually?" James asked.

Caroline shook her head. "He believes the fight will get worse and that it could drag the country into war." She was only repeating what she had heard spoken in the shop, but once she had said the words out loud, they seemed terribly ominous.

"Goodness, what are you two talking about?" Zilpha cried.

Caroline realized that everyone was watching them, and she felt herself blushing again.

"We're discussing what's happening in Kansas Territory," James said.

"Whatever for?" Zilpha asked, sighing loudly.

"My dear sister, some of us are interested in discussing more than the latest fashions, isn't that right, Caroline?" James said, turning to give Caroline a wink.

Caroline found herself smiling, but when she glanced up at Zilpha, the smile froze on her lips. Zilpha was watching her, and she suddenly looked a good deal like her mother, haughty and cold.

"Well, I for one would rather enjoy this beautiful day than discuss such morbid things," Zilpha said. Her face brightened. "I propose a game of croquet!"

"Capital idea," Ned cried.

James turned to Caroline. "Do you like croquet?"

Everyone seemed to be waiting for a response, so Caroline found herself nodding and saying, "Yes," even though she did not know what croquet was. As soon as she had said it, she felt silly. Why had she answered yes, when she should have answered no?

"Follow me then," Zilpha said, and they all headed for the door.

As they walked down a long marble hallway toward the back of the house, Caroline caught hold of Millie's arm. "Oh, Millie," she whispered. "I am embarrassed to ask, but what is croquet?"

"It is a game: You try to hit a ball with a wooden mallet," Millie whispered. "Don't worry. Just watch me."

Outside, the lawn was lush and green with a rose garden on one side and a pretty gazebo sitting in the shade of an oak tree. James disappeared around the house for a moment. When he came back, he was carrying long

wooden mallets, a basket of balls, and little wire hoops. He and Ned and Ben divided the hoops and set about pushing them into the ground. Zilpha took up the mallets and handed one each to Louvina and Millie and Caroline.

"How shall we break up the teams?" Ned asked.

"Ladies against gentlemen!" Zilpha and Louvina cried together.

"All right then," James said. "Now, who should go first?"

"Ladies first, of course," Zilpha replied. She took up her mallet and placed one of the balls from the basket on the ground. With a loud *whack* she hit the ball and sent it rolling toward the first hoop.

"Good shot!" Ned said, when the ball came to a stop a few inches away from the wire.

Ned went next and then Louvina and then James and Millie. Caroline watched intently.

"Now you're up!" Millie whispered to Caroline when it was time for her to hit the ball.

Caroline dropped the ball at her feet the way

she had seen the others do; then she swung the mallet with all her might. The ball rolled speedily through the grass.

"It's in!" James called, turning to grin at her. "You didn't tell us you were an expert at this game!"

Caroline felt her heart racing. She could hardly believe she had made it through the hoop on her very first try. She decided that she liked croquet, and played with determination. Her next few shots were quite good, and then it was Ben's turn.

Caroline stood a little apart from the others, watching as the game progressed. Zilpha made a poor shot, and then came to stand beside Caroline.

"Now, Caroline, do you really care about the doings way out in Kansas Territory, or were you just showing off for my brother?" Zilpha asked in a low voice.

Caroline felt her face go hot. She looked to make sure James was far away. "I wasn't showing off," she said quietly. "My uncle thinks what is happening in Kansas is important, and I believe him."

"Pshaw," Zilpha replied. "My father says it's all a bunch of nonsense, and it will blow over soon enough."

Caroline bit her lip. She was surprised at how angry she suddenly felt at Zilpha's words. Maybe she *had* been showing off a little to James, but she did feel that her uncle knew what he was talking about. She took a deep breath. Mother always said to think good, calm thoughts when anger reared its ugly head, so Caroline thought about how pretty and neat the lawn was with its gazebo and rosebushes and flower garden. She was a guest here, and she made herself smile politely and say, "Perhaps your father is right, Zilpha."

"My father is always right," Zilpha said, chin in the air.

Millie suddenly appeared, Louvina beside her. "I declare, I adore your hoop," Millie cried. "I must have one for the Winter Ball. I simply must!"

Caroline was relieved that the subject had changed. "Well, you'd better have Mrs.

Samms start on one right away," Zilpha said. "She's very busy now that the winter season is almost upon us."

"I will make an appointment as soon as I get home," Millie declared.

"So will I," Louvina added.

"What about you, Caroline?" Zilpha asked, her eyes sweeping over Caroline's attire. Again Caroline was reminded of Mrs. Maddox. "Do you think your dressmaker could make you a hoop for the ball?"

"I'm sure she could," Caroline replied. She knew she should reveal that her mother made her dresses, but something kept her from speaking the truth. It was wrong, but somehow it felt good to have Zilpha think that she had a secret dressmaker. "I don't know if I will be going to the ball, though," Caroline added.

"Oh, but you must go to the ball," Millie cried. "We are all going."

"What's all this about the ball?" Ned asked. The young men had come to join the girls.

"Caroline doesn't know if she is going to the ball," Millie replied.

"Nonsense," Ben spoke up. "All pretty young ladies must go to the ball, I decree it." He lifted his mallet as if he were a king and it was his scepter.

"Perhaps Caroline has more important things to do that night," Zilpha said slyly. "Perhaps she likes to attend abolitionist meetings instead of dancing."

Caroline felt a tightening across her chest. She did not want to look at Zilpha. "I like to do both," she found herself answering.

"A modern young lady!" James grinned at her, and Caroline found herself smiling back. It was strange. Deep down she knew she was not really so very modern. And she knew she would probably choose dancing over an abolitionist meeting any day. But she felt cross with Zilpha, and for some reason, she enjoyed feeling that James approved of her.

Iced In

Over the next few days, there was much talk of the ball, as first Louvina and then Millie got fitted for their new dresses with hoops.

Caroline felt torn inside. She wanted to ask her aunt and uncle if she could go to the ball, but she also did not want to bother them. Even if they said yes, going to the Winter Ball obviously meant wearing a special dress. Although Caroline's dresses were lovely, she knew they were not good enough. And she could never write to Mother and ask for the money for a new dress.

So Caroline tried not to be envious of her new friends and she tried not to let Zilpha's behavior at tea bother her too much. Zilpha was prickly, Caroline was discovering. Even to her old friends, Millie and Louvina, she could be friendly one day and sharp-tongued the next. Caroline felt most at ease when she was alone with good-natured Millie. And she felt happiest when she was studying.

"Think, think, think!" she often told herself. Miss Towbridge's words had become a phrase she repeated to herself whenever she became stuck on a particularly difficult problem.

"Think, think, think!" she told herself when she came home from her walks with the girls to sit at her desk and pore over her books.

"Think, think, think!" she told herself when she woke up early in the morning to study before her walk to school.

Caroline found it especially easy to think, think, think in Miss Howe's class. They had begun to read Shakespeare, and even though the words were sometimes difficult to follow, they made Caroline's heart sing when Miss Howe read them aloud.

Her heart did not sing in mathematics or in natural science, but she found the subjects interesting. And she tried to give her best in calisthenics, even though she often felt awkward and a little silly.

"Let yourself move freely!" Miss LaRue intoned. "Let your arms bend like the branches of a willow tree."

"It is too cold to do anything but shiver," Zilpha mumbled under her breath one day.

As the weather grew colder, Miss LaRue kept the giant windows open wide to let in the "fresh air." Many girls walked around with the sniffles all day long, but Miss LaRue only repeated, "Ventilation, ventilation, ventilation! Breathe deeply, young ladies! Breathe deeply!" when she heard any complaints.

Aunt Jane had said that winter came quickly to Milwaukee, and she was right. A sharp wind whipped off the gray lake and rushed in between the buildings, and by the middle of October, there was a dusting of snow on the city streets. Caroline brought out her flannels and her coat and muffler. Inside her uncle's house it was cozy, but outside and in the cavernous rooms of the college, she never felt completely warm despite the layers she put on. The air was always tinged with damp, and that seemed to make the cold more penetrating.

By the end of October, the snow had settled in. One night there was an ice storm. The wind howled and the ice tapped at the windows. In the morning, Caroline awoke to a silent, white world. There were no hawkers on the street. There was no movement outside at all.

"We're iced in," Nora said when she brought in the pitcher of water. "Winter is truly upon us now."

"I do not think you can go to school today," Uncle Elisha said at breakfast. "I am quite certain classes will be canceled."

Caroline looked mournfully out the parlor window at the all-white world. She hated to miss school, even for one day.

"Do not worry," Aunt Jane said, seeing the disappointment on Caroline's face. "The street cleaners will be out shoveling the snow and salting the roads soon enough. You will be able to go tomorrow."

After breakfast, Caroline went downstairs to the print shop with Uncle Elisha. All morning, she worked on her lessons at the table near the window. She glanced up now and then to watch the progress of the street cleaners as they shoveled pathways through the snow.

By afternoon, folks were venturing out. Packs of children raced up and down the street, throwing snowballs and pulling toboggans and sleds toward the bluffs by the lake. Watching the boys and girls made Caroline miss her brothers and sisters terribly. She thought of how they always played together in the snow and how snug the little house could be when everyone was inside during the winter months.

"Shall we take a walk?" Uncle Elisha asked, checking his pocket watch. The print shop was strangely empty. None of the men who usually came to talk had arrived yet that day. "I could use a little stroll."

Caroline dashed upstairs to get her coat and muffler. She couldn't wait to go outside. When she came back downstairs, Uncle Elisha and William and Johnny were throwing snowballs at each other in front of the house. The scene reminded her of snowball battles at home, and she boldly rolled a snowball before anyone noticed her and threw it at Johnny.

"Good shot, cousin!" Johnny laughed, and playfully threw one back at her.

"Let's head for the lake," Uncle Elisha suggested.

Together they made their careful way down the street. Caroline kept slipping a little on the ice, but William and Johnny were both there to catch her.

When they got to the bluff overlooking the lake, it was crowded with children on their sleds and toboggans. The lake itself was a blanket of white. Far off in the harbor, the tall masts looked like trees that had gone bare for the winter. The majestic ships sat in the icebound lake, caught like flies in a spider's web. Caroline tried to see if the *Milwaukee Belle* was among them, but she could not make out any of the names written on the hulls.

"What will happen to the ships?" Caroline asked.

"They stay frozen there till spring thaw," Uncle Elisha replied.

"Did the ship captains know they would get caught?"

Uncle Elisha nodded. "Many make their final runs with their cargo knowing they'll winter here."

Now that they were iced in, Caroline assumed that the city would go to sleep like a hibernating bear. But in fact it seemed that the city became even more lively during the winter months.

"No one wants to stay home," Aunt Jane explained one evening.

The streets were crowded day and night with all manner of sleighs and cutters rushing at top speed. Many attached little bells to their sleighs, so there was a constant ringing in the air. Children stayed out until dark sledding and tobogganing. Ice-skaters of all ages swooped

up and down the frozen river in between the tall buildings.

Caroline borrowed ice skates from Alice, and on Saturdays she went out with Millie and Louvina and Zilpha. She was used to ice-skating with a dozen or so townsfolk at the millpond at home, but here the river was clogged with skaters.

One Saturday afternoon William and Alice took Caroline to watch an iceboat race on the lake. The spectators stood on a platform near the harbor. The iceboats were low and flat and long enough to hold a half dozen men. Each had one sail that moved back and forth to catch the wind.

"Now watch, Caroline!" William said. "Those boats go quick as lightning."

In a moment, a gunshot sounded and the race had begun. The boat crews dashed along the ice, pushing their boats in front of them, and then all at once they hopped on board. It took a moment for the sails to find the wind, but when they did, the boats whipped across the icy plane. Faster and faster they went until

Caroline wondered if they would ever be able to stop.

The boats followed the shoreline for about a mile, and then they whipped around and came rushing back toward the harbor. Men began to shout, cheering for the captains of the boats.

"McNulty's got it!"

"Go, Huxley!"

"Come on, Cabbot!'

"Go, go, go!"

In a flash there was a winner, although many of the men loudly disputed who had won.

"McNulty was over the line first, for sure!"

"No, it was Cabbot!"

At last McNulty's boat was declared the winner. William wrote it down in a little notebook he took out of his breast pocket.

"So much for the Young Man About Town to report on nowadays, I must keep track," he explained. "Tonight there's a dramatic exhibition to attend."

"Would you like to join us?" Alice asked Caroline. "Aunt Margaret is watching little Billy, and we are going out."

"Grand idea!" William cried. "Charles Dickens is on the bill tonight. Should be quite enjoyable."

"Charles Dickens is here in Milwaukee?" Caroline asked. She had borrowed one of his novels, entitled *The Adventures of Oliver Twist*, from the schoolteacher last year and had raced through it.

"No, I'm afraid not," William replied with a laugh. "But a Mr. Abbott, an actor all the way from New York, will be reading from one of Mr. Dickens's novels."

Caroline hesitated. "I don't know if I should. I have a lot of schoolwork to do."

"Oh, please come along!" Alice begged. "Theatricals are so much fun."

"And educational to boot," William added. "After all, you do study literature in that college of yours, do you not?"

"Yes, we do," Caroline said, laughing.

"It is settled then. Be ready by six thirty!"

That evening Caroline went to her first dramatic exhibition. It was in the Town Hall, near the courthouse.

"Everyone is out tonight," William said as he took Alice and Caroline by the elbows and steered them through the wide double doors and into the crowd of people.

Chairs had been set up in rows before a raised stage, and everyone was trying to find a seat at once. Finally, William was able to secure three seats together, and Caroline sat, waiting for the night to begin.

At the ringing of a bell, a hush fell over the audience. Everyone stopped their chatter and sat up taller in their seats, watching the stage expectantly. In a moment, Mr. Abbott made his entrance, bowing deeply to the room's applause. He was tall and striking, with jet black hair slicked neatly back and a large black mustache that curled up at the ends.

"Good evening, ladies and gentlemen," he said in a deep, melodious voice. "I shall endeavor to entertain you with scenes from *David Copperfield* by Mr. Charles Dickens."

Mr. Abbott pulled from his breast pocket a fat leather volume, opened it, and began to read. "'Chapter One. I am born.'" He paused, and there was a ripple of laughter. "'Whether I shall turn out to be the hero of my own life, or whether that station will be held by anybody else, these pages must show.'"

At home, Caroline's family often took turns reading out loud for entertainment after supper in the evenings. But Caroline had never seen a professional actor before. She was amazed at how Mr. Abbott could make his voice sound like a young boy's one moment and that of a girl or an old man or woman the next.

An hour seemed to pass in the blink of an eye, and Caroline could hardly believe it when Mr. Abbott closed the book and bowed to the tumultuous applause.

"Is that all?" Caroline asked Alice.

"Are you disappointed with your first theatrical?" Alice looked surprised.

"No!" Caroline exclaimed. "I just want to hear the rest of the story."

"Well, you'll hear more of it after the intermission. But I'm afraid there isn't time to hear the entire story," William said. "We'd be here all night long!"

William led the slow way toward the back of the room through the crowds. Punch was being served, and once they had their glasses, they sipped the fruity drink and watched the crowd swirl about them.

"Greetings, Caroline!"

Caroline turned to see Zilpha. She was wearing her beautiful blue hoop dress. James was beside her dressed in a crisp black suit.

"Isn't Mr. Abbott wonderful?" Zilpha asked. "I just love theatricals, don't you?"

"Yes," Caroline answered. "I mean, this is the first one I've been to."

"The first?" Zilpha cried. "Goodness. Don't they have theatricals in your little town? Whatever do you do for fun?"

Caroline thought of how Mr. Kellogg, the mayor of Concord, had organized an evening of entertainment last year around New Year's. There had been a spelldown, and recitations by some of the scholars, and singing. It had been a lot of fun, but Caroline knew it probably wouldn't sound like much to Zilpha.

"I'm sure there are plenty of things to do,

Zilpha," James said, giving Caroline a warm smile.

"Well, there aren't any theatricals, that's true," Caroline replied, encouraged by James's words. "I wish there were. I am enjoying this one very much, and I know my family would too." She turned to introduce her friends to Alice and William.

"A pleasure to meet you!" James said when he found out that William worked at the newspaper with his father. "I've told Caroline how much I admire the *Register*."

James asked William about the newspaper business while Alice and Zilpha talked of other theatricals they had seen. As Zilpha chatted, Caroline noticed that her gloves were black lace instead of cotton. Caroline glanced down at her plain white cotton gloves and her same blue serge, feeling suddenly drab and unfashionable. Right away she was cross with herself. She had adored the blue serge before meeting Zilpha.

"And do you like to read Charles Dickens as

much as your cousin does?" James turned to ask Caroline.

This time Caroline didn't hesitate. "I've read only one of his books, but I liked it a great deal."

"Which book?" James asked, and after Caroline had told him, he nodded enthusiastically. "Ah, yes, that's one of my favorites!"

Caroline watched his handsome face. It was strange how different brother and sister were. Zilpha could be sharp and quick to judge. She often made Caroline feel keenly that she was a country girl, not a city girl. But James made her feel at ease, even though she had met him only twice.

A little bell sounded. "That means intermission is over!" Zilpha cried. "Hurry, we must get back to our seats!"

"Good evening, ladies." James bowed to Caroline and Alice, and took his sister's elbow. Caroline noticed Zilpha having trouble making her way back through the crowd with her full skirt. Finally, when everyone was settled, Mr.

Abbott strode out upon the stage, and once more Caroline became completely wrapped up in the story.

Caroline was quiet on the way home, savoring the evening. She had been in Milwaukee for over two months, but still it was hard to believe that she was really in a city, going to such wonderful events.

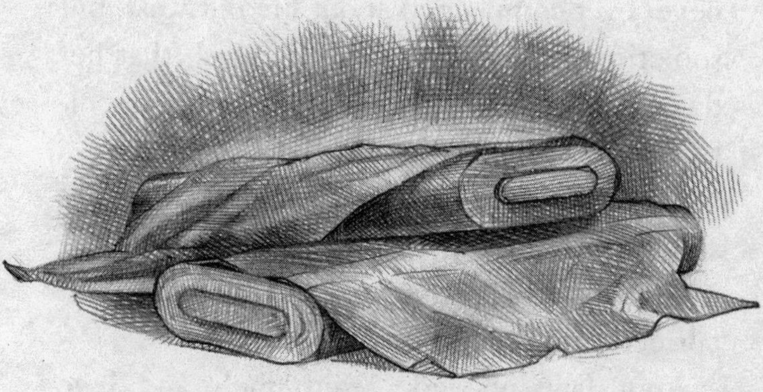

Hasty Preparations

Caroline went out frequently in the evenings with William and Alice. They heard a concert of music by Johann Sebastian Bach, and attended an exhibit of paintings from France.

Sometimes Caroline worried she was not paying enough attention to her studies. But she wasn't falling behind in her classes, and she remembered how Mother had sometimes talked of her life as a young lady back east. There had been parties and dances and concerts and plays to go to in Boston. Mother never ever complained about life out west, but sometimes she had expressed a wish that her daughters could experience some of the culture she had known as a girl.

One evening, Aunt Jane asked Caroline if she'd like to attend the Winter Ball.

Caroline was not sure she had heard her aunt correctly. "The Winter Ball?"

Aunt Jane nodded. "Your uncle and I go every year, and so do Alice and William and Johnny. It is quite the social event of the season."

Caroline's heart seemed to skip a beat.

"I assume you would like to attend the ball with us?" Aunt Jane asked.

Caroline felt herself nodding. She still could not speak.

"Well, then, we must see about a dress for you right away. I will make an appointment with my dressmaker as soon as possible."

Now Caroline felt something sinking within her. She could never afford a new dress. Her thoughts raced, and she began to speak very quickly. "I could rework my green wool so that it will be nice enough for a dance. I could put some more flounces on the skirt and rework the sleeves a bit. I am not as good a seamstress as Mother, but I know I could work quickly."

Aunt Jane searched Caroline's face for a moment. "Your mother certainly has taught you to be a practical young lady." Aunt Jane paused. "Your dresses are lovely, Caroline, but I do think something a little finer is needed for the Winter Ball, my dear."

"I cannot afford a whole new dress, Aunt Jane," Caroline said solemnly.

"Your uncle and I would like to buy you a dress," Aunt Jane said, and when she saw the look on Caroline's face, she quickly continued, "Your mother never let us help after your father passed away. I know buying you a new dress is rather small compensation. But still, your uncle and I would like to do it."

Caroline bit her lip. She wanted very much to give in, but she kept thinking of what Mother would say. Mother would never want her to accept such an expensive gift as a dress, even from her aunt and uncle. Mother never liked to be beholden to anybody.

Aunt Jane seemed to sense what she was feeling. "Caroline, I have never had a girl to dote on. It would give me great pleasure to spoil you just a little."

Caroline felt her resolve melting. Perhaps it would be rude to refuse Aunt Jane's kind offer. She hesitated a moment longer, and then she came up with an idea.

"Perhaps I could do some chores in exchange for the dress, or I could help Nora in the kitchen. I could cook for you and Uncle Elisha. I am a good cook. Mrs. Hotchkiss says so."

"I am sure you are a good cook." Aunt Jane laughed. "As a matter of fact, Nora has asked for a few days off at Christmastime to visit her sister. Perhaps you could do a little cooking then."

"Oh yes!" Caroline cried.

"'Tis settled then!" Aunt Jane said brightly.

Caroline rushed to Aunt Jane and hugged her.

"Thank you. Thank you so much, Aunt Jane," she whispered.

"You are quite welcome, my dear," Aunt Jane said, holding her back a little after the hug. "You are quite a treasure to have for a few months. I only wish it were longer!" Aunt Jane smiled and then released Caroline. "Now hurry along to school, and I shall make the proper arrangements."

Caroline thanked her aunt again and then hurried to meet her friends. She did not tell them about going to the ball. She wanted to hold it close, her own precious secret, all day long.

Aunt Jane had told Caroline that she would pick her up after school the next day and they would go to Mr. Schmidt's dry goods store to buy material for the dress.

"Mr. Schmidt has the largest store in all of Milwaukee, and he always has the latest fabrics to choose from," Aunt Jane had explained. "And then we have an appointment with my dressmaker."

After school, Aunt Jane took Caroline to Germantown. It was a part of the city where many German families lived.

"You will hardly hear any English here," Aunt Jane said after they had crossed the river.

Now Caroline noticed that all the signs in front of the shops were written in both English and German. And she heard German being spoken from every corner as they drove down the street and stopped in front of a tall two-story brick building with "Schmidt & Co." written on the glass windows. Inside, Caroline could hardly believe her eyes. The store took up both floors of the building. It was much bigger than any general store Caroline had ever seen.

The first floor held all manner of household goods and tools and furniture and dry goods. A sign pointing up to the second floor listed ready-made clothing and shoes and toys and sundries.

"Ah, Mrs. Quiner! How happy I am to see you!"

A man came rushing down one of the crowded aisles toward them. Caroline recognized him as the German man she had seen in the print shop on her first day. "How can I help you today, ma'am?"

"Good day, Mr. Schmidt," Aunt Jane replied. "This is my niece Caroline." Mr. Schmidt made a little bow. "We have come to find some material for a dress to be made for her for the Winter Ball."

Mr. Schmidt's eyes lit up. "Ah, I have some wonderful ready-made dresses from New York. They are quite magnificent."

Caroline's heart leaped inside her chest. She wanted to see the ready-made dresses, but Aunt Jane shook her head. "I thank you for your kind suggestion, Mr. Schmidt, but I am old-fashioned. I already have an appointment with my dressmaker, and I would like to choose some fabric to bring to her."

Mr. Schmidt bowed his head. "Of course, Mrs. Quiner. I have the finest fabric anywhere. It arrived from New York just before the freeze. Right this way."

As they followed Mr. Schmidt to the back of the store, Aunt Jane whispered to Caroline, "I know the ready-made dresses are said to be acceptable, but I adore my dressmaker, Mrs. Samms."

Caroline let out a little gasp. "Mrs. Samms is your dressmaker?" she asked.

"Yes, my dear, she is wonderful," Aunt Jane replied.

"I know—I mean, my friends all say so," Caroline said, feeling giddy.

Mr. Schmidt went behind a counter and began to take down bolt after bolt of beautiful fabric for Caroline and her aunt to admire. There were soft silks and shimmery satins and intricate brocades and fine wools and delicate organdies and the thinnest of muslins. Besides the cloth, Mr. Schmidt had dainty lace and yards and yards of tulle and boxes of shiny buttons to choose from.

"Oh I do like this lavender silk," Aunt Jane said, draping some over Caroline's shoulder.

Caroline liked it too. She knew her friends' ball dresses would be made out of silk or satin, but something took hold of Caroline, and she found herself trying to see the choices as her mother would see them. A dress made by a dressmaker was a special gift. Caroline knew it would have to last her a long time, long after she left Milwaukee with its sophisticated Winter Ball. She knew she needed a dress that would wear well, no matter what the occasion, no matter where she might be.

"What about this?" she asked, reaching for a bolt Mr. Schmidt had just brought down from the shelves.

"Oh, the delaine," Mr. Schmidt said, unfurling a swath of deep shimmery green. "It is a muslin. Very popular back east. Very fashionable and light."

Caroline took the material between her fingers. It *was* light, but it felt durable too. And it shimmered magnificently when she turned it this way and that. Over the deep green, there was a faint pattern of red, like tiny strawberries.

"I do like the silk, but this would be quite becoming on you," Aunt Jane admitted, holding the delaine up and cocking her head to one side. Then she caught up a swath of blue-and-cream-colored cotton that shimmered. "This is lovely, too, you know. The blue matches your eyes."

Mr. Schmidt brought out a mirror and held it so that Caroline could look at the material draped over her. Both pieces of cloth were very beautiful, and they both seemed practical as well.

"I don't know which I like better." Caroline sighed.

"Well, then, we shall take both!" Aunt Jane announced.

"Oh!" Caroline gasped, startled by Aunt Jane's words. She wanted to protest, but Mr. Schmidt was already hurrying to cut several yards from the bolts of cloth, and she didn't want to seem rude in front of a stranger.

"Now let us choose some trimmings to go with these," Aunt Jane said.

So they chose shiny red buttons to go with the delaine and green velvet ribbon for trimmings. For the blue and cream, they chose blue buttons and dark blue lace.

Then Mr. Schmidt showed them an assortment of gloves. "My wife says these are very popular with the young ladies," he said. He laid out several pairs of stylish lace gloves, just like the ones Caroline had noticed Zilpha wearing.

"Oh, they are darling," Aunt Jane cried. "Go ahead, Caroline. Try them on. The black lace would go with your dresses."

Caroline slipped the gloves over her fingers and held up her hands for inspection.

"They are lovely," Aunt Jane said. "Don't you think so?"

"Yes, I do," Caroline breathed. She could not utter a word as Aunt Jane added them to the pile of goods she was purchasing.

"Now then, what else can I do for you ladies?" Mr. Schmidt asked.

"Hmmm." Aunt Jane looked thoughtful and then reached down and lifted Caroline's skirt an inch to peek at her shoes. "Perhaps you have some shoes, Mr. Schmidt?"

"Oh, yes, come right upstairs. The finest ready-made shoes anywhere!"

Caroline felt a knot in her stomach tightening, and she bit her lip. But Aunt Jane fixed her with a determined look, and Caroline somehow knew it would be impossible to protest. They followed Mr. Schmidt upstairs, and he brought out several shoes to look at, some made of brocade and others made of the softest kid.

"How about these?" Aunt Jane asked, choosing a pair of black leather ankle boots that buttoned fashionably up the side. "Practical and pretty too." She gave Caroline a knowing look. "That's what you prefer, isn't that right, my dear?"

Caroline nodded and slipped on the pretty boots. The boots fit so perfectly, she felt like crying. She had never in her life owned a pair of brand-new shoes. As she walked a little about the room, it was as if she were walking on air.

"That should do it," Aunt Jane said. She told Caroline to look around while she finished up her business with Mr. Schmidt.

In a daze, Caroline walked up and down the aisles. She wondered what Mother would say when she returned with a trunk full of new clothes. She knew Martha would be jealous. She came to a row of ready-made dresses hanging from a long metal pole and carefully looked through them. The dresses were all satin and silk and brocade and tulle and lace. They were indeed magnificent, as Mr. Schmidt had said, but Caroline knew Mrs. Samms would make her a dress every bit as lovely.

After the aisle of dresses, Caroline came to two whole rows of dolls. The dolls were all different sizes—some three feet tall and some as tiny as a finger. Some were made of porcelain with fancy lace dresses and some were made of carved wood with simpler gingham clothes. They were all standing or sitting in their boxes on the shelves, staring wide-eyed at Caroline. Even though Caroline was much too old to play with dolls, it was still something to see so many pretty dolls in one place. She thought of how much Lottie would love one of these dolls. Because of her aunt and uncle's generosity, she hadn't spent much of the money her mother had given her.

The prices were displayed on tags next to each doll. Caroline looked through them all and finally chose a wooden doll, six inches high, with painted blue eyes and a smiling pink mouth. It cost two dollars. Then she chose two velvet ribbons for Eliza and Martha, one blue and one green, for a nickel each, and a ten-cent paper of needles for Mother because Caroline knew Mother would want a practical gift. For Pa she chose a clever little brush for cleaning his pipe that cost a nickel, and sticks of peppermint for the boys at a penny apiece.

Mr. Schmidt totaled everything up for Caroline when she was ready. Her Christmas gifts came to two dollars and twenty-eight cents, and she felt quite grown-up as she counted out the coins and gave them to the storekeeper.

"Your uncle and I were planning to send a Christmas package to your family anyway," Aunt Jane said. "So we can put our gifts together, and Elisha will send it by post."

"Thank you," Caroline said. "Thank you for everything, Aunt Jane."

Aunt Jane fluttered a hand in the air. "It is my pleasure, truly," she said.

Mr. Schmidt added up Aunt Jane's purchases and made a note in a thick black ledger. Then he wrapped everything in brown paper and carried the packages to the buggy.

"So good to see you, Mrs. Quiner, Miss Quiner!" he called as they drove away. "Please come again!"

"Now we must hurry to Mrs. Samms's shop!" Aunt Jane said. They crossed the river again and headed toward the shop Caroline had visited with her friends.

This time the shop was open. Mrs. Samms came to greet them right away and take their wraps. The dressmaker reminded Caroline of an older Nora. She had the same bright green eyes and beautiful red curly hair, only Mrs. Samms's hair was piled stylishly high atop her head, with little ringlets falling about her small face. Delicate gold drops dangled from her earlobes. She wore a red pincushion stuck full of pins on a band around her wrist, and there was a tape measure about her neck.

"How wonderful to see you, Mrs. Quiner," Mrs. Samms said, and then, "So nice to meet you, Caroline," after they had been introduced.

"It is nice to meet you, too," Caroline responded. "I've stopped to look at the dresses in your windows. They are beautiful."

"Why, thank you," Mrs. Samms said. "Now, please come this way."

Caroline and Aunt Jane followed her through another room, where two girls who looked about the same age as Caroline sat sewing. One was in a chair near the window, hunched over some careful needlework. The other girl sat in front of a strange, black, humming machine. The girl was pushing a pedal with her feet and carefully guiding a piece of sky-blue satin over a little table under the arm of the machine.

"Is that a sewing machine?" Caroline asked, and Mrs. Samms nodded.

"Yes. I call it my little helper. It is a miraculous invention. Worth every penny. Cuts our sewing time in half."

Mrs. Samms continued on to the next room. Caroline lingered a moment longer watching the girl and the machine. The girl glanced up and smiled shyly, and Caroline smiled back. She had heard about these newfangled sewing machines, and she also knew that they were terribly expensive, but she knew Mrs. Samms must be right. They would be worth every penny if it meant half the time sewing.

Mrs. Samms settled Caroline and Aunt Jane into two comfortable chairs around a little table and brought out a book of drawings to show them.

"Since you admired the dresses in the window, I assume you would like a hoop?" Mrs. Samms asked, flipping the pages to a drawing of two dresses like the ones on display.

Caroline took a deep breath and glanced at Aunt Jane. "I do admire the hoops a great deal, but I will be leaving Milwaukee after school is over, and I am not sure they will be practical when I return home. Might I have a full skirt without a hoop?"

Mrs. Samms looked surprised for a moment. "Goodness, you are a thoughtful young lady, are you not?"

Aunt Jane said proudly, "Yes, she is."

Mrs. Samms flipped through some pages. "Let's see. We could fix you up with a crinoline, which is not as wide as a hoop but still gives us some fullness. And I will add several flounces to the skirt, so that it will appear fuller. How would that be?"

Caroline smiled and nodded. Aunt Jane brought out the material for Mrs. Samms to see. Then Mrs. Samms pointed to two drawings in her book. "These would be very becoming on you, I believe, and work with the fabric."

Both had tiny V-waisted bodices and full ruffled skirts and wide lacy sleeves. One had a deep scooping neckline that prettily framed the shoulders, and the other had a rounded neckline with lace decorating it.

"Oh, they are perfect!" Caroline breathed.

"All right then, let us begin!" Mrs. Samms said, clapping her hands together. "I think the delaine should be for the Winter Ball, and it should have the lower neckline. We will work on it first to make sure we have it for then. How about that?"

Caroline nodded, feeling a tingle of excitement.

"Now, if you would come with me."

Mrs. Samms led Caroline into a private dressing room so that she could remove her dress. Then the dressmaker took Caroline's measurements and jotted them down on a little piece of paper.

"That should do it," Mrs. Samms said at last. "Come back in two days' time for your first fitting."

And that was that. Caroline had been to her first dressmaker. As they headed home, Caroline asked Aunt Jane if her mother's shop had been like Mrs. Samms's.

"Yes, a bit like it," Aunt Jane said. "It was a small shop, but very fine. All the fashionable ladies stopped by for their fittings and to discuss the latest styles with Charlotte. She was busy all the time, and when she left, her clients were forlorn, let me tell you!" Aunt Jane sighed. "I often thought she could have done a wonderful business here, after your father's terrible tragedy."

Caroline was quiet, wondering what life would have been like if Mother had moved to the city instead of farther west. The first years in the woods near Concord had been very difficult. But everything had worked out for the best.

"Mother wanted to make sure we had our own land," Caroline said thoughtfully.

Aunt Jane nodded. "Your mother is a brave woman. I admire her courage to strike out on her own."

Caroline looked down at her gloved hands. Suddenly she felt very proud of her mother and very close to her, even though they were miles apart.

Over the next few weeks, Caroline was very busy. There were dress fittings to go to, and schoolwork to keep up with, and even dance lessons.

Caroline had been to parties at home, of course, but she had never been to such a formal ball, and she had never really danced as a young lady. Aunt Jane wanted to make sure she knew how to waltz and polka.

"And there is the quadrille, of course, and

the Virginia reel is usually played toward the end of the dance," Aunt Jane said.

Each night after her schoolwork was done, Caroline practiced dancing with Aunt Jane in the parlor. Sometimes Uncle Elisha and Johnny and even Alice and William joined in. Caroline came to look forward to the hours after supper when they moved the furniture aside in the parlor and danced about the room.

"I'm not sure the ball will be as much fun as this," William said, laughing.

"And you'll not find such a good dance partner as me!" Johnny joked.

Caroline was so wrapped up in the hasty preparations for the ball, she completely forgot about her birthday. One night the whole family gathered for a wonderful surprise supper, and afterward Nora appeared at the table with a beautiful double-layer cake with chocolate icing.

"Happy birthday!" they all called.

After they had eaten the scrumptious cake, Uncle Elisha presented her with a leather-bound copy of Charles Dickens's *David Copperfield*.

"Now you will be able to read it all to your heart's content," William said.

"Oh, thank you," Caroline cried. She ran a hand over the leather cover. "Oh, thank you, thank you!"

There was also a letter from home wishing her well on her special day. Everyone had written a line.

"We all miss you terrible!" Thomas had written in his untidy hand.

"We like your letters," Henry had jotted down. "The city sure sounds like fun."

"Martha says you are a city girl now and we will hardly know you," Eliza had carefully written.

"That is not true!" Martha wrote. "We can hardly wait for you to come home and tell us everything—and do your fair share of the chores!"

Caroline laughed out loud. She could almost see her sister's peeved expression.

Finally, Mother had written in her beautiful script, "It is hard for me to believe that you are really sixteen years old now. I am so proud of you, Caroline. We send this letter with our love and best wishes for a happy birthday away from home."

Caroline felt her eyes welling with tears of happiness. She too could hardly believe that she was really sixteen years old. She had been away from home for three months and she had become accustomed to life in the big city. Soon she would be attending her first ball.

Winter Ball

Hours before the ball was set to start, Caroline began her preparations. First she took a warm bath. Then she dusted herself from head to toe with some of her aunt's fragrant powder. She put on her new stockings, her clean shift, and the crinoline, and buttoned up her new shoes.

Nora came to help with her hair. They had decided the night before to curl it. Nora heated the curling tongs on the stove. She rolled Caroline's hair carefully in brown paper and then clamped the tongs down.

"You don't have to worry about curling your hair, do you, Nora?" Caroline asked as Nora worked.

"Why, no, miss," Nora said, laughing. "My sister always said I could use this mess as a bird's nest."

"I think your hair is so pretty!" Caroline cried.

"Well, it's not as thick and long as yours, that's for certain. You'll be able to sit on yours soon enough."

The curling took some time, but finally it was done and Nora stood back to admire how nicely the curls fell.

"Shall we put the front part up and leave the rest down?" Nora asked, and Caroline nodded. She thought of how pretty Zilpha had looked when she had worn it that way.

Now that her hair was done, Nora helped with the corset. She pulled at the stays until Caroline was breathless.

"You know what they say." Nora laughed, giving a final tug. "A young lady's waist should match her age."

"Thank goodness I am sixteen now instead of fifteen!" Caroline replied, giggling a little. "I am not sure I could stand one more inch!"

Caroline knew Miss Beecher would never approve, but she did not care. Tonight she would choose fashion over comfort.

Nora helped Caroline put on her best frilly petticoat over the crinoline, and next came the beautiful delaine. Nora tugged and straightened and pulled until she declared that everything was just right.

"Oh, miss, come see how pretty you are!" she exclaimed, leading Caroline to the mirror.

Caroline did not think she was vain, but as she gazed at her reflection, she felt happy. The dress was beautiful and fit perfectly. The scalloped neckline framed her small shoulders, and the wide bell sleeves fell in lacy ruffles to her elbows. The tight V-shaped bodice made Caroline's waist look almost as slender as Zilpha's, and the skirt flared out magnificently with row after row of flounces that Mrs. Samms had made out of a lighter green material and draped and trimmed with knots of the dark-green velvet.

Caroline lifted the skirt a little and pointed a toe. She had borrowed some lovely cotton stockings from Alice, and her new boots were dainty and smart. They made her feet look tiny.

She dropped her skirt and looked at herself again in the mirror. She decided to take a left-over piece of velvet ribbon Mrs. Samms had given her and tie it about her neck.

"Just right, miss!" Nora exclaimed. "I wish you all the best tonight. I know you will have a fine time."

"Thank you, Nora," Caroline said. Then she put on her new lace gloves and made her careful way down the stairs, holding her wide skirt up a little so she would not trip.

In the parlor, Aunt Jane was helping Uncle Elisha with his cravat. Aunt Jane was lovely in plum-colored satin, and Uncle Elisha looked handsome in a crisp white shirt and a black cutaway jacket with black trousers.

"Oh, my dear!" Aunt Jane exclaimed when she caught sight of Caroline. "How beautiful you look!"

Uncle Elisha held out his hands so that Caroline would take them, and then he stood looking at her for a moment in silence. “I wish your father were here to see you,” he said finally in a quiet voice.

Caroline felt tears welling up again.

“Just one more thing to complete your ensemble,” Aunt Jane said. She went to her room and came hurrying out, then pulled Caroline to the mirror. “May I?” Caroline nodded, and her aunt carefully pinned something on the green ribbon around Caroline’s neck.

Caroline looked in the mirror and saw that it was a beautiful gold pin, flat and long and wide with scalloped edges.

“Oh, it is perfect, Aunt Jane! Thank you!” Caroline exclaimed.

Aunt Jane gave Caroline her long black velvet cloak to wear for the evening with its warm hood. Downstairs, Johnny had already brought the sleigh around.

“You will save the first dance for me, then, cousin?” he asked as he helped her into the buggy.

"Of course I will!" Caroline laughed.

Johnny took the reins, and they went dashing through the streets. The moon was shining bright and round overhead, and it made the icebound city seem to shimmer.

Johnny headed toward the Milwaukee Gardens. The ball was being held in the dance hall on the far end of the park. The paths had been cleared of snow and ice, and little round globes of light illuminated the way.

Johnny escorted Caroline while Uncle Elisha took his wife's arm. There were other couples strolling along the lighted path. Caroline caught sight of silks and satins and jewels flashing under the lamps. She felt like a character in a storybook or a play. It did not seem possible that she was really here and dressed so finely.

As they neared the grand hall, Caroline heard soft music playing. The music grew louder as they went up the stairs and entered the tall doors.

Inside, the room was so bright and sparkly that after coming in from the dark, Caroline had to blink a little. The high ceiling seemed to be made of gold, and the walls were a soft blue like the sky. Lamps made of cut crystal hung above the gleaming parquet floor. Elegant ladies and gentlemen walked among marble statues and tall ferns. A small orchestra played on a raised platform.

Caroline stood with her aunt while the men took their wraps to the cloakroom. She felt her heart beating very quickly, and she knew she was flushed pink with excitement.

No one was dancing yet. The room buzzed with talk and laughter. Caroline gazed at all the handsome gentlemen in their crisp suits and all the ladies in their beautiful ball gowns. The skirts were all wide, but Caroline was glad to see that not every lady wore a hoop.

Aunt Jane gave polite waves of recognition and pointed out the important people to Caroline as they arrived through the doors. There were prominent businessmen and city council members, and the mayor and his wife made a grand entrance.

"I do wish Margaret had come." Aunt Jane

sighed. "But she never likes to dance, and of course she enjoys minding little Billy." Aunt Jane's face lit up. "Oh, good, here come Alice and William now!"

Alice looked wonderful in a pink, off-the-shoulder muslin gown with flower garlands, and William was handsome in a black suit.

"There are quite a few eligible bachelors lurking about," Johnny observed, then he gave Caroline a wink. "I think Caroline will have her pick of dance partners this evening."

Caroline pretended to give him a stern look, but she glanced about the room and noticed that there did seem to be a large number of young men in attendance.

"Isn't that your friend?" Aunt Jane asked, and Caroline turned to see Millie waving a gloved hand in the air.

"Oh, Millie, you look so pretty!" Caroline said when Millie had made her way through the crowd. Millie's dress was a lovely rose-colored silk with frothy tulle draped at her shoulders and in scallops around her skirt. Her blond hair fell in perfect ringlets about her flushed face.

"So do you, Caroline!" Millie replied. She introduced her mother and father.

"How do you do?" Mrs. Roberts said. "We have heard a great deal about you. And of course we already know your aunt."

As the Robertses began to chat with Aunt Jane and Alice, Millie took Caroline's hand. "Let's go look for Zilpha and Louvina, shall we?"

Aunt Jane said it was all right, and the girls took a tour about the room. When they came to the long tables holding the refreshments, Millie said, "Oh, all these pretty cakes and cookies! Everything looks delicious, but I could not eat a thing, my corset is so tight."

"So is mine," Caroline whispered back.

"What would Miss Beecher say?"

"Well, I won't tell her, will you?"

The girls giggled.

"There they are!" Millie said, taking Caroline's hand again and pulling her across the room.

Zilpha and Louvina were standing together, chatting and watching the crowd. They both looked very stylish in their satin ball gowns with their wide hoops. Zilpha's dress was pink and Louvina's was blue, and both skirts had so many tulle flounces, Caroline thought they looked like puffy clouds in the sky.

"Good evening, good evening!" they all called to one another brightly.

Zilpha quickly looked Caroline up and down. "Your dress is quite fetching, Caroline, even if it isn't a hoop," she said.

Caroline took as deep a breath as she could in her corset. For some time, she had felt dishonest because she was holding back the truth from her friends. "Mrs. Samms made it," she announced.

"But what about *your* dressmaker?" Zilpha asked.

"My mother made my other dresses," Caroline confessed, feeling better right away. "She was a dressmaker in Boston before she came west."

"Oh, how convenient," Zilpha said, her voice becoming cool and haughty.

Caroline felt a flash of anger, but immediately

she calmed herself. She would not let Zilpha ruin her first ball.

"Yes, it is convenient," she said simply.

Zilpha looked away. "Oh, good, there are the boys!" she cried, waving a lace handkerchief in the air.

Ned and Ben and James appeared out of the crowd. "Good evening! Good evening!" they called. They were dashing in their black cutaways and neat gray trousers. Their hair had been slicked back from their clean-shaven faces.

"How lovely you ladies are this evening," Ned said.

"Lovely indeed," Ben added.

"So, Caroline, you are making good on your statement that you like to dance as well as attend meetings?" James asked, his eyes twinkling. Caroline knew instinctively that he was not making fun of her. Again she thought of how different brother and sister were.

"I do hope there will be some dancing soon!" Zilpha spoke up.

As if the conductor had heard her words,

the music changed and the orchestra began to play a stately waltz.

Ned immediately turned to Zilpha and bowed. “May I have this dance?”

Zilpha nodded happily, and Ned took her hand and led her out to the dance floor with all the other couples assembling there. Caroline watched Ben ask Louvina to dance. She thought she saw James turning toward her, but then she felt a tap on her shoulder.

“You promised the first dance to me, remember?”

It was Johnny. He held out his hand and Caroline took it gratefully. She realized as he led her out to the dance floor that she was a bundle of nerves. Her legs were stiff beneath her, and she felt a little dizzy. She knew she wanted to dance with James, but she was glad to dance her first waltz with her cousin.

“Here we go!” Johnny said, taking Caroline in his arms and waltzing her around the room.

Caroline’s legs still felt stiff and awkward. She glanced at all the beautifully dressed couples gliding effortlessly by, and then she tripped a little over Johnny's toe. Johnny caught her and continued to twirl her about the room.

"Just imagine yourself back in the parlor, and you'll do fine," Johnny whispered.

Caroline pictured herself inside the comfort of her uncle's home, instead of inside such a grand hall, and she felt herself relax.

"Now you're getting it, cousin!" Johnny cried happily.

Around and around they went. Caroline began to enjoy the music and the swirling motion. By the time the waltz came to an end, Caroline knew she wanted to keep dancing.

After one more waltz, Johnny led her back to her friends and Caroline introduced him around.

"Are you in the newspaper business yourself, then?" James asked.

"No," Johnny replied, and explained about his clerkship.

"I didn't know you had such a handsome cousin," Millie whispered in Caroline's ear.

When the music started up again, James

immediately turned to Caroline. "May I have this dance?" he asked.

Caroline nodded, her stomach tightening into a knot. As he led her onto the dance floor, she willed herself not to trip over someone as handsome and sophisticated as James. In a very short while, however, Caroline felt herself relaxing. It was obvious that James was an excellent dancer, and so he was an excellent partner. His movements were smooth and graceful, and Caroline felt suddenly gay and carefree as they whirled about the room.

"Are you enjoying your time in Milwaukee?" James asked as they danced.

"Oh, yes," Caroline said. "It is going awfully quickly."

"Perhaps you will like it so much, you will stay on in our fair city," James replied.

"Well, I hope to get a teaching position closer to home," Caroline said.

"Surely there are more teaching positions in the city than in the country?" James asked.

Caroline was quiet for a moment. She had never thought about it before, but of course

James was right. There were likely to be more teaching positions in Milwaukee, and they probably paid more than teaching positions in the country. But then, she would not be able to live at home.

"I don't think I could be this far away from my family," Caroline finally said. She knew she must sound like a little girl, but she couldn't help it.

"But you have family here," James commented.

"Yes, but I would miss my mother and my brothers and sisters."

James asked about her home, and Caroline told him a little bit, but the waltz soon came to an end. Caroline found herself wishing that James would ask her to dance again, but Ben was standing before her.

"Can't monopolize this young lady's time, Maddox!" Ben cried laughingly.

Caroline enjoyed dancing with Ben, but she did not really know what to talk about. She had never talked with him outside the group and did not know what his interests were.

They ended up discussing how lovely the music sounded, and then she danced with Ned and with James again. She felt a little breathless from all the dancing, and she found herself thinking of Miss LaRue and calisthenics. She wondered if Miss Beecher approved of dancing as a form of exercise.

"A penny for your thoughts," James said, and Caroline smiled and quickly shook her head. She felt too shy to talk to James about calisthenics, so she asked him about his classes at the university instead.

"My favorite class is literature," James told her.

"I like literature too," Caroline cried.

"I would like to be a writer," James confessed. "That is why your uncle's business interests me so. But my father does not think it is a proper profession."

"I suppose being a writer is a hard life," Caroline said.

"Yes, but it is a noble profession," James said enthusiastically, and then his expression changed to a frown. "Sometimes I think what my father does—buying and selling land at a profit—is rather unscrupulous."

Caroline did not know what to say. She was surprised by how cross James seemed all of a sudden. She was glad when he grinned again and shook his head. "Never mind. We must not discuss any serious matters at such an occasion." He laughed, and Caroline joined in. "Perhaps I will come see your uncle's print shop sometime, as you suggested."

"I'm sure he wouldn't mind," Caroline said.

The next dance was a quadrille, and Johnny came to claim her. And then she danced with William and then with Uncle Elisha.

"Goodness, your dance card has been full!" Uncle Elisha joked, his eyes twinkling down at her as he brought her back to Aunt Jane and the rest of the family. "Aren't you tired?"

"A young lady never tires of dancing," Aunt Jane said. "Why, when I was Caroline's age, I never could sit still when dance music was playing."

"Yes, I remember!" Uncle Elisha said,

chuckling. "It took some gumption to keep up with you."

Aunt Jane gazed back at him lovingly. "Well, let's see if you can keep up with me now, old man." She held out her hand.

"Old man, indeed!" Uncle Elisha laughed, taking his wife's hand and jauntily leading her to the dance floor.

The orchestra had launched into a lively polka, and Caroline watched as her aunt and uncle began to three-step around the room. She found herself suddenly brimming with love and admiration. Her aunt and uncle were such a happy, generous couple. She was glad for the chance to get to know them better.

The rest of the evening rushed by in a swirl of music and dancing. Caroline hardly sat down the whole evening. A few of the bachelors Johnny had pointed out asked her to dance, and she could not refuse out of politeness. She noticed that Millie always had a partner as well.

"Isn't this fun?" Millie asked when they had

a moment alone together. Then she gave Caroline a coy look. "I've noticed that James has danced more dances with you than with anybody," Millie said. "And I heard him tell Ben that you were a sensible girl."

Caroline glanced at her friend in surprise. "Oh, well, it's just we both like to study literature," she explained, feeling flustered. "And he's interested in my uncle's newspaper."

"In any case, he is quite handsome." Millie said. "Your cousin is, too. I do hope he will ask me to dance again."

As if he had heard Millie's wish, Johnny appeared with James beside him.

"Wouldn't want to leave two such pretty ladies in the lurch," Johnny said, bowing before Millie.

After what Millie had said, Caroline felt awkward with James again. She wondered if he had really called her sensible, and if he meant it as a compliment or not. She supposed he might think her sensible because she read books and wanted to be a schoolteacher. She found herself wondering if he thought she was pretty as well, but she knew that was just vanity jumping in where it wasn't wanted.

Caroline was so caught up in her own thoughts, she forgot to make small talk, but James did not seem to mind.

They waltzed in silence until the music ended. Somewhere a clock struck the hour.

"Is it really midnight?" Caroline asked in surprise. She had never stayed up so late before.

"Yes, and the ball is over," James said.

"Oh!" Caroline cried, disappointment washing over her. Somehow she had believed the ball would go on and on.

James led her back to her family and bade her good night. She waved good-bye to Millie and Louvina, but she did not see Zilpha. As Johnny drove home through the moonlit streets, Caroline closed her eyes, wanting to hold on to every glittering moment of the wonderful evening.

At home, Nora was waiting up for Caroline to help her out of her corset and dress.

"Please tell me all about it, miss," Nora begged.

So Caroline told her all about the lovely dresses and the handsome gentlemen and the dancing.

"Ah, it sounds grand!" Nora sighed.

"It was," Caroline replied.

After Nora had gone, Caroline fell into bed. In the dark she could still see the sparkling ballroom and all the skirts whirling, whirling, whirling. Deep in the night, she was still dancing in her dreams. And then the dream changed and she was rushing over the ice on an iceboat, going faster and faster and faster, rushing past streets and faces and trees. She was rushing through the woods, past her home. She thought she heard her sisters calling, but she was going too fast to stop.

The Winter Season

"Now scholars, I do wish you all a happy Christmas. I hope your holiday is merry, and I will see you in the new year."

Miss Howe stood at the front of the classroom, gazing fondly at all the young ladies before dismissing them for the winter holiday. As Caroline filed out behind Millie, she placed a little gift on Miss Howe's desk alongside all the other scholars' offerings to their teacher. Caroline had made Miss Howe a clove apple, wrapped it in brown paper, and tied it with a red bow. She hoped Miss Howe would like it.

Outside, snowflakes flurried into the air. The girls set out on their final walk home for the fall term, pulling their mufflers and cloaks tighter about them against the chill.

"Three whole weeks!" Millie cried once they were away from the school.

"I am sorely glad to have a rest from lessons," Zilpha added.

"So am I!" Louvina said.

Caroline was glad too, even though she did not want to admit it out loud. She had received high marks in all her classes, but it had been a struggle, especially toward the end, when she had been distracted by the outings and by preparations for the ball. She was happy for the chance to put away her books for a time and not have to think, think, think.

"Christmastime is always terribly busy," Millie said. "I am looking forward to dancing again, aren't you, Caroline?"

Caroline nodded, feeling a tingle of excitement. Aunt Jane had already mentioned that there was a Christmas dance and a New Year's

Eve dance to attend.

"The dances are not so fine as the Winter Ball, mind you, but they are fun all the same," Millie continued. "I do hope your cousin comes along with you, and I know James will want to dance with you again." Millie giggled and gave Caroline a little nudge with her elbow.

Caroline glanced at Zilpha, wondering what she would say, but Zilpha was working at a button on her glove and appeared not to have heard. "I am particularly glad to have a rest from school so that I don't have to cook anything for a while," she said.

Louvina and Millie quickly agreed with her, but Caroline kept quiet. Nora was leaving that very night, and Caroline was looking forward to doing the cooking in order to repay at least some of her debt to Aunt Jane and Uncle Elisha.

When the girls reached the corner of Jefferson and Division Streets, they called good-bye and went their separate ways. Back home in the quiet, tidy kitchen, Caroline sat for some time poring over Miss Beecher's recipe book. She decided that she particularly liked the recommendation that "In winter, the breakfast and teatable can be supplied by a most inviting variety of muffins, griddle cakes, drop cakes, and waffles made of rice, cornmeal, and unbolted flour, all of which are very healthful and very agreeable to the palate." She checked the supplies of flour and rice and cornmeal, sugar and molasses, and decided that she would make sure there was always something tasty on hand during the holidays.

In the morning she woke up very early and lit the stove and started the coffee going. Then she made hotcakes and fried salt pork.

"Goodness, what is that delightful smell?" Johnny asked, poking his head around the corner.

"Go into the dining room, and you will find out soon enough," Caroline teased. She felt at ease with Johnny, because he reminded her of Henry. She was glad his law firm had closed for the holidays so she would see more of him.

Caroline stacked the hotcakes on a tray,

drizzled them with butter and maple syrup, and covered them with a cloth so they would stay warm. Then she took out the dishes and asked Johnny to help her set the table.

"Yes, ma'am," Johnny said, giving her a salute.

Everything was ready when Aunt Jane and Uncle Elisha came through the door.

"Good morning!" Caroline cried. "Please have a seat, and I will serve you."

"And what have we here?" Uncle Elisha asked.

"My, how wonderful this all looks!" Aunt Jane exclaimed.

"Jane mentioned that we would have a new cook," Uncle Elisha said laughingly, "but I had no idea she would be so efficient!"

Caroline dished out the hotcakes and salt pork and then waited anxiously as her aunt and uncle and cousin took their first bites.

"Delicious! Simply delicious!" Uncle Elisha cried. "These are the best hotcakes I've ever tasted."

Johnny held out his plate for more as his way

of complimenting Caroline. "Lucky the man who marries you, cousin! You're sharp as a tack and a good cook to boot."

Caroline gave Johnny a scolding look, but her cousin grinned and she had to smile back. "I am glad I came to Milwaukee," she said suddenly.

"We are too, my dear—we are too," Aunt Jane replied heartily.

"Especially now that you are going to feed us!" Johnny joked.

And Caroline did feed them. Over the next few days she cooked the dishes she had learned from Mother, like chicken pie with a flaky crust and chicken and dumplings and roast beef with brown gravy and fried potatoes and beef stew and corn bread with cracklings. And she made sugar cookies and little white sugar cakes for tea.

She also tried new dishes from Miss Beecher's recipe book. She made codfish balls and baked ham, and she tried several hearty soups. Miss Beecher was particularly fond of preparing various kinds of hash as a way to economize, and so Caroline made hashes out of the leftover chicken and beef. Everyone in the household declared them quite tasty.

In between her cooking duties, Caroline also helped Aunt Jane decorate for Christmas. They made a wreath of holly and ivy for the front door, and they made more clove apples to set about the house and to give as Christmas presents.

Uncle Elisha and Aunt Jane had begun the custom of keeping a Christmas tree, and so one evening Uncle Elisha brought a tall fir home and placed it near one of the windows in the parlor. The whole family sat together stringing cranberries and popcorn into long garlands to drape on the boughs of the tree. Caroline baked cookies and made warm spiced apple cider, and everyone complimented her on the treats, especially little Billy.

"More!" he kept calling, and then "More, *please*," when his mother corrected him.

"It's so cozy here," Caroline said in a quiet voice after the tree had been decorated and everyone sat quietly gazing at it.

"Well, don't get used to it." Aunt Jane

sighed. "The coming week will be quite hectic, I'm afraid."

Caroline soon learned how true this was as the aunts took her along with them to holiday teas and a holiday concert and she went with her friends on a sleighing party. And there was a Christmas dance as well.

"Father should give you your own column," Johnny teased Caroline as she rushed about. "Young Lady About Town."

The Christmas dance was held in the Town Hall. Caroline wore her blue-and-cream-colored dress, and once more she danced nearly every dance. She tried not to put too much store in what Millie had said about James. It did seem that he liked dancing and talking with her, and he was handsome and nice, as Millie had pointed out. But Caroline did not really think he liked her in a special way. After all, he was a dashing university man who came from a rich family. He could have his pick of young ladies, and Caroline was still only sixteen—just a girl, really.

On Christmas Eve, the whole family joined

in a caroling party. The merry group walked from house to house, singing Christmas carols. Caroline knew some of the songs, but sometimes she simply listened to the voices around her. Her favorite was "The Holly and the Ivy."

> *"The holly and the ivy,*
> *When they are both full grown,*
> *Of all the trees that are in the wood,*
> *The holly bears the crown."*

At each house, the carolers were invited inside after singing and given treats, like buttery popcorn balls and hot apple cider and cakes.

"You see, we sing for our supper," Johnny told Caroline.

"Isn't this a jolly way to spend Christmas Eve?" Alice asked.

Caroline nodded. It *was* jolly, and it was also interesting to see how other folks lived. Some homes were very grand, with marble foyers and rich carpets and beautiful paintings on the walls and servants to serve the guests. Other homes were modest, but they were clean and cozy and comfortable.

On Christmas morning Caroline settled into the kitchen to begin the preparations for the Christmas meal. She stoked up the fire in the fireplace and lit the stove and dressed the goose that Nora had ordered.

Once the goose was roasting, she made hotcakes and salt pork again because Uncle Elisha had declared that it was his favorite breakfast. She had just finished setting the table when the front door opened and little Billy shouted at the top of his lungs, "Happy Christmas, happy Christmas! Santa Claus brought me a new sled!"

William and Alice and Aunt Margaret greeted Caroline warmly, and then Uncle Elisha and Aunt Jane and Johnny came downstairs.

"Happy Christmas, happy Christmas!" they all called, embracing one another.

Caroline admired Billy's new sled, which he had insisted on bringing with him.

"Mama says there are more presents here,"

Billy said, looking hopefully up at his grandmother.

"That is right, my sweet," Aunt Jane said, "but first we will eat breakfast and then see what is under the Christmas tree."

"Oh, the whole house smells wonderful already!" Alice said, helping Caroline dish up the food.

After they had eaten, the grown-ups could not keep little Billy from the Christmas tree any longer. They followed as he rushed upstairs and exclaimed over a set of wooden toy soldiers lined up on the floor and a long wooden boat with a white canvas sail.

"Christmas is always more fun with children around, don't you think?" Aunt Jane asked with moist eyes. Caroline thought of her own family opening their gifts back home in Concord. How she wished she could see Lottie's face when she caught sight of the little doll Caroline had sent.

"Now it's the grown-ups' turn!" William declared, passing out the wrapped gifts from under the tree.

Uncle Elisha had given Aunt Jane a beautiful silver brooch, and Alice had received little gold earrings from William. Aunt Margaret was pleased with some new false sleeves Aunt Jane had made for her to replace her old ones and a crocheted tea cozy and a book of poems by Wordsworth. Johnny had received a new vest and a new cravat to wear to the office, and both Uncle Elisha and William had been given shiny new black felt hats.

From home, Caroline had received a new muffler and a clean new notebook and a pair of woolen stockings. Thomas, who had become quite good at woodworking, had carved her a likeness of her dog, Wolf. Caroline's heart felt heavy as she looked at the tiny wooden figure. Wolf was a very old dog now, and Caroline realized guiltily that she had not thought of him much in all her rushing about here in Milwaukee.

When Caroline opened her gift from Aunt Jane and Uncle Elisha, she could hardly believe her eyes. Nestled in the tissue paper sat the beautiful pin Aunt Jane had lent her for the Winter Ball.

"It was your grandmother's," Aunt Jane said. "I know she would want you to have it."

Caroline felt the tears coming, and she rushed to her aunt and uncle and hugged them close.

"Thank you so much," she whispered. "Thank you for everything."

Then Caroline brought out her own small gifts for her Milwaukee family. She had made clove apples for Alice and Aunt Margaret, and she had bought handkerchiefs for William and Johnny and Uncle Elisha and embroidered them with their initials. For Billy she had knitted a pair of red mittens from yarn in Aunt Jane's yarn basket, and for Aunt Jane she had carefully copied out a poem by Whittier and crocheted a pretty frame for it.

"How clever!" Aunt Jane exclaimed.

Caroline knew her gifts were not so fine, but she meant the Christmas feast to be part of her offering. Soon she went back to the kitchen to finish her preparations. She allowed Alice to help her, but she would not let the aunts do any work.

"This is my day to cook!" she announced.

She mashed the potatoes and leeks, and she stewed sweet potatoes and made a cranberry sauce. When the goose was ready, she made a thick gravy from the drippings. She had baked her special Christmas bread the day before, and a dried apple and raisin pie. Alice had brought muffins spiced with almonds and cardamom, and a lingonberry tart. She helped set the table with Aunt Jane's good linen tablecloth and good china dishes.

"Look at this table!" Uncle Elisha exclaimed after Caroline had called them down. "I've been smelling the food cooking all morning and am simply ravenous now! This is the juiciest goose I've ever seen!" he cried as he began carving.

After they were all seated, Uncle Elisha said the prayer and then passed the dishes of food. The room was completely silent as everyone began to eat, and then the whole family was talking at once.

"Delicious!"

"Best Christmas dinner ever!"

"The dressing is so tasty."

"The goose just melts in the mouth!"

Caroline's heart swelled with pride as she dished out second and third and fourth helpings. The family ate and ate until one by one they announced that they were too full to eat another bite. Caroline was glad that the first Christmas dinner she had cooked on her own was such a success.

A Special Announcement

"Hello, young ladies," Miss LaRue greeted the class. "We shall resume our calisthenics. I hope you continued to practice them over the holidays."

Caroline and Millie glanced at one another and stifled their giggles. They had not done any calisthenics, but they had certainly been active. They had ice-skated and taken sleigh rides. And they had gone to a New Year's Eve dance at which the bells had rung in 1856. It had been a wonderful three weeks. She did not think that she would ever forget her winter season in Milwaukee.

Now that school had resumed, everything was turned around. Calisthenics was the first class of the day and then there was domestic arts. In the afternoons they continued where they had left off in their studies with Miss Compton, Miss Towbridge, and Miss Howe.

"Miss Beecher feels that routines should be changed in order to keep us sharp," Miss LaRue explained.

Caroline was happy to be back at school. She felt refreshed from her time away, and now she was ready to think, think, think once more. The first month went quickly by, and at the start of the second month, Miss Mortimer gathered the whole school together for an assembly.

"I have a special announcement to make," Miss Mortimer said, looking as giddy as a young girl. "I have just received a letter from Miss Catharine Beecher. She will be joining us for graduation week in order to observe our progress here at Milwaukee Female College."

A murmur of excitement went through the

room. Millie grabbed Caroline's hand and squeezed. It would be quite something to meet such an important person as Miss Catharine Beecher.

"This is wonderful news indeed," continued Miss Mortimer, "and it will give us the opportunity to demonstrate to Miss Beecher how very much we appreciate her guidance. I am recommending that every class organize a special project in honor of her. I want Miss Beecher to see how very well you all are doing as scholars and as young ladies."

Miss Mortimer ended the assembly, and all the scholars hurried back to their classrooms, chattering together about what Miss Beecher might look like and which classes she would prefer.

"Isn't it wonderful?" Miss LaRue asked when calisthenics class had been called to order. "I shall endeavor to create a special routine that incorporates our daily repetitions. And of course I must begin right away, for we have only four months to practice before graduation!"

Caroline could hardly believe it. Only four months left of school! Only four months left in Milwaukee. Time had moved very quickly.

Now the whole school was in a frenzy to make sure they were prepared for Miss Beecher's visit. In domestic arts class, Miss Hotchkiss announced that they would cook a special meal for Miss Beecher. In mathematics, the scholars would stand at the blackboard and work through problems Miss Compton gave them. In history and geography, they would give a history of the world, with each scholar presenting her own portion. In Miss Howe's class, each scholar would write a special composition.

"The best composition will be chosen to be read out loud by the author at the graduation ceremony," Miss Howe announced. "Now, I have written topics on slips of paper and put them in the basket sitting on my desk. As you leave today, please take a slip of paper."

After Miss Howe had dismissed class for the day, all the scholars filed by her desk. Caroline heard laughter and little whispers of surprise as one by one the girls opened their slips of paper to see what their assignments would be.

"The railroad!" Zilpha cried. "I have to write about the railroad! What a noisy, dirty thing to have to describe!"

"Tradition! How in the world can I write about tradition?" Millie asked, turning to Caroline. "Oh you must help me!"

Louvina's slip of paper read "America," and Caroline thought that would be a perfect topic to write on. Anxiously she opened her own, excited to see what her topic would be. But when she read the two words written in Miss Howe's delicate hand, she felt disappointment wash over her.

"What does yours say?" Millie asked.

"The ocean," Caroline answered. "I have never seen the ocean. Have you?"

All the girls shook their heads. For once, Caroline did not feel that Zilpha was more sophisticated.

Caroline walked home with the girls and said good-bye at the usual corner. She was lost in thought as she reached the print shop. The door opened as she passed, and she was surprised to see James standing there.

"Good day, Caroline," he said, tipping his hat. "I suppose it is nearly good evening. I've been in your uncle's shop so long, I've lost track of time."

"Oh, did you come to see the newspaper being printed?" Caroline asked.

"Yes, I did!" James replied enthusiastically. "Your uncle made a formal invitation at the New Year's Eve dance, and I took him up on it today." His eyes were bright and his face was flushed with excitement. "It certainly was fascinating watching the presses and listening to all the talk. And look here, your uncle gave me some things to read," James said. "It is interesting stuff."

James held out some pamphlets and handbills. Caroline saw that they were some of the abolitionist material Uncle Elisha printed.

"I'm glad you came to see the print shop," Caroline told him. "Mondays are always busy, since they print the newspaper for the next day."

"Yes, I saw with my own eyes how busy it was." He looked down at the handbills. They were silent for a moment, and then James said, "Well, I am certain I will see you very soon. Your uncle told me to come back anytime, and I plan to!"

"That would be nice," Caroline replied.

James tipped his hat again. Caroline watched as he walked off down the sidewalk. When he reached the corner, he turned and waved, then disappeared.

Caroline went into the print shop. Inside, the machines were humming and everyone was busy. Uncle Elisha was having another heated discussion with Mr. Smitty in the back. Caroline had grown used to the way her uncle had to bully the man to finish his stories. William was working at one of the presses. Aunt Margaret was sitting at her desk, but she had just paused in her typesetting.

"Ah, how was school today?" Aunt Margaret asked when she caught sight of Caroline.

"Miss Beecher is coming for the week of graduation!" Caroline announced.

"Oh, how thrilling!" Aunt Margaret exclaimed. "It will be an honor to meet her."

Then Caroline told Aunt Margaret about the composition she had to write.

"Well, I'm not the writer in the family," Aunt Margaret said. "You should get your uncle's advice."

When Uncle Elisha came to give Aunt Margaret a story to typeset, Caroline showed him the slip of paper and told him about the assignment.

"How can I write about something I've never seen?" she asked.

"Well, I will wager that your teacher wants you to use your imagination, Caroline," Uncle Elisha said. "You've read about the ocean in books, I'm sure, and our own great lake is not so very different. Vast and unpredictable. Maybe you could make a study of the lake when the ice has cleared."

Uncle Elisha's advice was sound. That night Caroline asked Aunt Jane to tell her about the ocean, and she also tried to recall books she had read that might be helpful. She felt a little better about her topic, but still the next day she decided to speak with Miss Howe. In between classes she went to Miss Howe's room and found her sitting at her desk.

"I've meant to thank you for the clove apple you gave me at Christmas," Miss Howe said. "It was a lovely gift. It made the rooms I'm renting seem so homey!"

Caroline had never thought about her teacher's life once she left the school at the end of the day.

"You don't live with your family?" Caroline asked timidly. She didn't want Miss Howe to think she was impertinent asking about her life.

Miss Howe smiled and shook her head. "No, my family lives farther north. I came to Milwaukee to be a schoolteacher, and I rent rooms nearby."

"Are there many teaching positions in Milwaukee?" Caroline asked, remembering her conversation with James at the Winter Ball.

"Yes, there are," Miss Howe replied enthusiastically. "Milwaukee is growing bigger every day. There are more schools being erected as we speak." Miss Howe searched Caroline's face. "I know your goal is to be a teacher when you graduate, Caroline, and I am very pleased with your progress here. There are no teaching positions at the college at present, but you could speak to Miss Mortimer about the future."

Caroline's mind raced. She knew Aunt Jane would love her to stay on in Milwaukee, and if she had a teaching position, she could pay a little money for her rent and she could send the rest home. But then she thought of her brothers and sisters, especially of little Lottie.

"I am hoping to get a teaching position closer to home," Caroline said at last.

"Yes, I understand." Miss Howe's voice was kind. "It's not easy to leave one's family. But I must admit I've grown rather fond of city life."

Caroline imagined that Miss Howe had many friends in Milwaukee, and perhaps she attended concerts and theatricals and meetings just as the aunts did. It was probably an exciting life.

"Of course, there may not be any teaching positions near my home," Caroline said hesitantly. "I suppose I could always come back to Milwaukee if I could not find work."

"If you do, Miss Mortimer would always make time to meet with you, a former scholar here, and I would enjoy seeing you again as well. You have been a pleasure to teach these past few months, Caroline. You are a diligent scholar."

"Oh, thank you," Caroline said happily. "I have enjoyed your class so much."

"Now then," Miss Howe said, "what can I do for you today?"

After Miss Howe's compliment, Caroline felt a little sheepish as she explained that she was having trouble knowing how to begin writing her composition.

"Imagination!" Miss Howe said, sounding like Uncle Elisha. "I want you to exercise your mind just as you exercise your limbs in calisthenics. You are an excellent writer, Caroline. All your compositions have been first-rate. I have every confidence that you will rise to this challenge."

After hearing Miss Howe's encouraging words, Caroline did see it as a challenge rather than a burden. Each day, before school and after it, she sat at her desk and tried to write. She made several good starts, but she could never get past the first few sentences. Twice, she walked by herself down to the lake for inspiration, but it was still covered with ice and snow.

"Oh, well. I have plenty of time," she told herself.

Awakening

One Saturday afternoon, Caroline finally went to an abolitionist meeting with Uncle Elisha and the aunts. The meeting was held in a small church across the river. The narrow room was crowded with men and women. Uncle Elisha passed out the handbills he had printed, while the aunts found a place to sit among the packed pews.

Caroline sat, eagerly waiting for the meeting to begin. Uncle Elisha had told her that this was a particularly important meeting because a freed slave would be speaking. Caroline had read Frederick Douglass's narrative about his life as a slave, but she had never seen a slave with her own eyes.

Finally, the meeting came to order. A Mr. Randall reported on the current state of Kansas Territory. "It is a battlefield, ladies and gentlemen," he announced in a voice that trembled with emotion. "A battlefield. I have seen the terrible bloodshed with my own eyes."

After Mr. Randall, Mr. Jackson was introduced. Mr. Jackson was the freed slave. He was a small, wizened man, with skin the color of brown leather. He stood and eloquently told of the terrible cruelties he had suffered at the hands of his "master." He had finally escaped to the north, where his master had tracked him down. But the family with whom he had found refuge was able to buy his freedom. At the end of his speech, Mr. Jackson turned and lifted his shirt to show the marks on his back from his many whippings.

Several ladies in the audience gasped, and one of them fainted straightaway and had to be carried outside to be revived in the cold air. Caroline felt tears stinging her eyes. She could not understand how one human being could be so cruel to another.

As Caroline was leaving the meeting with her family, she caught sight of James in the crowd. When they were outside, James approached her uncle and thanked him for telling him about the meeting.

"I wish my father would come to a meeting," he said angrily. "My father thinks that all abolitionists are radical. But it is not radical to think that all men should be free!"

"Amen, brother," someone close by said, and Caroline nodded her head in agreement.

After the meeting, James seemed to spend all his free time in the print shop. When Caroline came home in the late afternoons, she would see him sitting in the back with the other men, listening to their talk. Sometimes he would come and chat with Caroline for a little while before returning to the circle of men. He began to write short articles for Uncle Elisha under the name "New to the Cause."

"James is a good writer," Uncle Elisha told Caroline. "He has a way with words."

As the weeks passed, Zilpha did not mention reading James's articles, but Caroline assumed that she must be proud of her brother. One day Caroline brought a copy of the *Register* to show the girls, because there was an article on hoops. Next to that story was a piece by James.

"My uncle says James is quite talented," Caroline said, pointing to it.

Zilpha's dark eyes suddenly flashed with anger, and she pushed the newspaper away. "You know, Caroline, my father is not pleased with James's going to your uncle's office. He does not approve of James's writing these silly pieces."

Caroline felt her own temper flare, but she worked to control it. Finally she said as pleasantly as she could, "They are not silly pieces. James is writing about important matters. My uncle says—"

"I do not care what your uncle says!" Zilpha cut her off. "My father says James is wasting his time at that print shop." Zilpha turned on her heel and walked away.

Louvina glanced at Caroline and then hurried to follow Zilpha.

"Oh, dear!" Millie said. "Zilpha can be short-tempered. But I'm sure she didn't mean to sound so . . . harsh." Millie patted Caroline's arm. "I'm sure this will all blow over."

But it did not blow over. Day after day, Zilpha remained cold to Caroline. They continued to walk to and from school together in their foursome, but Zilpha was quiet and did not speak directly to Caroline, and neither did Louvina.

Caroline felt angry, but she tried to be polite, as Mother had schooled her to be in every situation. Even so, the questions whirled around inside her head. What harm did it do for James to spend his spare time at the print shop and write articles, especially when the articles were about such important topics as slavery? It was not Caroline's business, and it wasn't really Zilpha's either. James was a man of nineteen, after all. He could do as he pleased.

One day, a week after Zilpha's outburst, Caroline was late coming out of domestic arts class because she had helped Miss Hotchkiss clean up. As she was about to turn a corner, she heard Zilpha speaking in a low voice and then she heard her own name. She stopped in her tracks and listened.

"Mama says that Caroline is setting her cap for James because he is so eligible," Zilpha said.

There was a pause. Caroline felt her heart speeding up. She knew she should leave, but she was rooted to the spot.

"I like Caroline," Millie said in a quiet voice. "I thought you liked her too."

"I like Caroline well enough," Zilpha replied in a flippant tone. "She can be charming, but she is certainly not good enough for James. Her family are homesteaders and her mother was a dressmaker. Plus Papa says her uncle is a radical and has put all kinds of radical views into James's head. He never cared so much about the slaves before. Now he spends all his time with Caroline at the print shop, and

I think she is contriving to get his attention."

Caroline felt as if she could not breathe. She turned and walked away as quietly as she could. When she found an empty classroom, she went in and closed the door, thoughts swirling.

How could Zilpha's mother think that she was "setting her cap" for James? How could Zilpha say she was "contriving" to get James's attention? How could they have such a low opinion of her?

Caroline thought back over the last few months, carefully examining her actions. Of course she had found James's attention at the dances and in the print shop flattering, but she had never really considered it to be any more than politeness and general niceness on his part.

Then she felt her wounded pride crying out. What if it had been more? It was terrible to think that the Maddoxes believed her family was not good enough because they were not wealthy.

Her eyes welled with tears of anger and self-pity, but she willed them not to fall. Mother always said eavesdroppers only learned things they did not want to know, and now Caroline knew Mother was right.

Taking several deep breaths, Caroline forced herself to push Zilpha's ugly words out of her mind. She lifted her chin and walked back down the hall to the next class. Most of the scholars were already at their desks, and Caroline took her seat beside Millie.

"Oh good, did you finish with Miss Hotchkiss?' Millie asked.

"Yes," Caroline answered. She was glad that she had an afternoon of lessons to keep her mind occupied. At the end of the day, Zilpha announced that her father was picking her up in his buggy.

"I'm tired of walking," Zilpha said. She would not meet Caroline's eye. "And now that the snow is melting, I don't want to get my skirts so wet and muddy."

Caroline was relieved. Louvina went with Zilpha, but Millie walked home with Caroline as if nothing had happened. Zilpha and Louvina had been entertaining, Caroline had to admit, but Millie was a true friend. She had defended Caroline, and she was standing by her. Caroline felt they would be friends even after Caroline had left Milwaukee.

As the weeks passed, Caroline threw herself into her schoolwork. She was eager to do well, but she was also glad to keep busy. Whenever she let herself think of the unkind words she had overheard, her skin burned. At school, however, she made a point of being nice to both Louvina and Zilpha. She did not want to give Zilpha the satisfaction of knowing that she had hurt her feelings. Deep down she wondered if Zilpha had listened for her foot-steps in the hallway before speaking, knowing she was bound to hear.

Soon the city began to thaw. The days turned warmer, and slowly the ice in the river and lake began to melt. Sometimes Caroline walked alone to the bluffs overlooking the lake, and she would hear a startling *crack!* as great chunks of ice split apart and drifted away.

One day she walked to the lake and saw that the schooners that had been frozen all winter long were awake and free at last. Two of them were heading out of the harbor, the wind full in their sails. It was thrilling to see them go, plowing through the sparkling water, sailing off on some new adventure.

Once more as she gazed out across the seemingly endless blue, she thought of her father. Her memories of him were hazy, but she realized that living in Milwaukee with Uncle Elisha had made her feel closer to him. She knew deep in her bones that if he had lived, he would have been kind and thoughtful and strong in his convictions, just like her uncle.

As a little girl she had been told that her father's ship had been lost in a storm on this very lake, but she had never been truly able to grasp what had happened to him. Being in Milwaukee had allowed her to understand what her father had faced each time he had left his family. Lake Michigan was beautiful, but it was also eerily vast and unpredictable.

Caroline shuddered even though the sun shining upon her face was warm. She pulled her shawl tighter about her shoulders and turned away from the shimmering water. When she reached home, she hurried upstairs to her desk. Her mind was racing with ideas. Taking out a clean sheet of paper and her pen and ink bottle, she began to write.

She described the calm and beauty of the ocean she could see in her mind's eye. She imagined a ship sailing upon that placid surface, all those on board cheerful. She then envisioned a sudden ferocious storm, the sailors helpless in the face of nature's unpredictable fury.

When she came to the end of the composition, she realized she was trembling. She glanced over what she had written, feeling surprised at herself. She carefully blotted the ink dry, took up the sheet of paper, and carried it downstairs to the print shop.

"What's this?" Uncle Elisha asked, looking puzzled as Caroline held the sheet out to him.

"It is the composition I wrote for Miss Howe's class," Caroline answered. "Would you mind reading it?"

"Of course, of course, my dear! It would be my pleasure!" Uncle Elisha took the paper and settled back into his chair.

Caroline bit her lip and clasped her hands, suddenly nervous, as Uncle Elisha's eyes drifted across the composition. Perhaps it had been impulsive to give it to Uncle Elisha. Perhaps she should have worked on it a little longer.

Finally, after what seemed like a very long time, Uncle Elisha looked up at Caroline. His eyes were moist. He cleared his throat before speaking.

"This is good, Caroline. This is very good. Quite dramatic and moving. I think your teacher will be pleased."

Caroline felt a warm contentment spreading through her, from her toes to the very tips of her fingers.

"Thank you, uncle," she said.

Best Wishes

"Can you believe school is nearly over?" Millie asked. "Oh, Caroline, I will miss you! Promise me you will write."

"I will miss you, too," Caroline said, and meant it with all her heart. "I promise I will write, and you must promise to return my letters!"

"Of course I will," Millie said. "And I still want to come visit you someday."

"That would be such fun. You could meet all my brothers and sisters then." Caroline was quiet for a moment, thinking of Lottie and how much her little sister would have changed in nine months. Certainly she herself had changed. She felt that she was stronger and more confident in new situations than she had been when she first came to Milwaukee.

"Hurry now, girls, find your places!" Miss LaRue cried, breaking into Caroline's thoughts. "Miss Beecher will be here any moment."

Millie let out a little squeal of excitement and grabbed Caroline's hand. They had already changed into their calisthenics costumes. Now they hurried into the line of girls all waiting for Miss Beecher to arrive to watch the calisthenics routine they had been practicing.

After Miss LaRue's class, the domestic arts class would prepare a meal for Miss Beecher's dinner. The next day, the other classes would give their oral presentations. And then the graduation ceremony would follow on Wednesday.

Caroline's stomach twisted nervously. Uncle Elisha's prediction that Miss Howe would like her composition had been right. Miss Howe had chosen "The Ocean" from all the other compositions to be read out loud, and Caroline would be reading it in front of the whole school. She was proud and excited and scared all at once.

"Line up quickly, girls!" Miss LaRue's voice again brought Caroline back to the classroom. Caroline watched as Miss LaRue fluttered about nervously, making sure the girls were standing straight and tall and that their costumes hung just right.

At last the door opened and a lady strode purposefully into the room, followed by Miss Mortimer. The lady wore an elegant black silk dress that rustled as she walked. Her dark hair framed a broad, handsome face.

Miss Mortimer said, "Attention, scholars. It gives me great pleasure to introduce Miss Catharine Beecher."

Miss Beecher's dark eyes surveyed the room. "Good morning, young ladies!" she called in a booming voice.

"Good morning, Miss Beecher," all the young ladies responded.

Miss Beecher brusquely strolled down the line, looking each girl in the eye as she passed. When she had reached the end, she turned on her heel and went back to stand beside Miss Mortimer. "It does my heart good to see a roomful of such strong, healthy-looking scholars!" she said.

Miss LaRue went forward. "We have prepared a special presentation for you, Miss Beecher," she said.

"Splendid!" Miss Beecher cried.

"If you would have a seat here, please," Miss LaRue said, indicating two chairs against one wall.

Miss Beecher and Miss Mortimer settled into the chairs, and Miss LaRue gave the girls a look of encouragement. She clapped her hands, and Miss Fleming began to play the piano.

Caroline counted out the first bar of music, and then she launched herself into the routine the class had practiced over the last few months. All down the line of girls, arms lifted, bodies stretched, feet moved in time to the lively tune. With such an important audience, all the girls gave their best, and Caroline did truly feel for once that she was as supple and as strong as a young sapling.

When the routine came to an end, Miss Beecher seemed very pleased. She smiled broadly and applauded as all the young ladies made little curtsies.

"Well done, Miss LaRue! Well done, young ladies!" Miss Beecher cried. Then she went to each girl, drumming her knuckles down their spines as Miss LaRue did each week. Caroline stifled her nervous giggles as she felt Miss Beecher's strong hands on her back.

"Good! Good! You appear to be in perfect health. I congratulate you!" Miss Beecher announced.

With that, she turned and strode out of the room, Miss Mortimer following close behind. Everyone breathed a sigh of relief, and Miss LaRue was ecstatic.

"How beautifully you performed!" she said. "I am so proud of each and every one of you!"

Now Caroline hurried to change out of her

calisthenics costume. She could hardly believe it was for the last time.

"What did you think of Miss Beecher?" Millie whispered as they were walking down the hallway.

"I thought she was a handsome lady," Caroline whispered back.

"Yes, I thought so too," Millie said, giggling a little. "She seemed very serious. I hope she likes our meal."

"I hope so too," Caroline said.

In domestic arts, the menu for the noontime meal consisted of roast beef, boiled potatoes, and rolls, with a salad of greens, and an apple pie for desert.

"Miss Beecher likes simple meals the best," Miss Hotchkiss had told them when she created the menu.

Caroline was in charge of the pie because she had been deemed the best pastry cook.

"Your crusts are always perfectly flaky," Miss Hotchkiss had told her, and Caroline had felt proud.

By noon the food was ready. Miss Beecher

sat at the head of the teachers' table, and the young ladies served her. When she had finished everything on her plate, Miss Beecher pronounced the meal perfectly done and healthful.

Caroline was relieved. She was glad the first day of Miss Beecher's visit had gone so well. She went home that evening tired from all the excitement of preparation, but feeling satisfied as well.

The second day went as smoothly as the first. Miss Beecher watched the scholars perform the mathematics problems Miss Compton gave them on the blackboard, and listened as they each recited their part of the history of the world.

"Well done! Well done!" Miss Beecher said at the end of the presentations. "I am glad to see that you are all bright, accomplished young ladies."

At last, the day of graduation arrived. Caroline slept fitfully. She had grown more and more confident of her abilities, but she couldn't help but feel nervous about standing before the entire school to read her composition. In the morning she took great care getting ready. She put on her blue serge and pinned her hair up. The whole family accompanied her to the assembly hall.

"Good luck!" they called as they took their seats. Caroline went forward and sat with Millie and the rest of her classmates.

Miss Mortimer brought the assembly to order and greeted the scholars and their families. She gave a short speech and then turned the program over to Miss Howe, who explained about the assignment she had made and how she had chosen the best composition to read here today.

Caroline felt her hands trembling. She was hot and cold all at once, and she was not sure she would be able to stand. Her legs felt weak.

"I now call on Caroline Quiner to come forward and read her composition entitled 'The Ocean,'" Miss Howe was saying.

Somehow Caroline made it down the aisle and up the platform to the lectern. She glanced at all the faces staring up at her expectantly. She could hear her own heart pounding, and her mouth was suddenly dry as dust. She willed herself to look down at the piece of paper she was holding, not at the sea of faces. She cleared her throat and began to read.

"What a world of beauty there is in the Ocean. Look upon it in a calm, and it fills us with awe and admiration. How it sparkles as the sun shines upon it in all its splendor, and how lovely and majestic the ships look sailing upon its smooth and placid surface."

As she read, her voice grew stronger. She felt her confidence building as she asked the audience to imagine a ship coming into port, with friends and relatives happy to see their loved ones home safe and sound.

"Then imagine a ship on the water in a storm. What a contrast! All is hurry and confusion on board; for many hands must be at work to save the ship if possible."

She read on, so caught up that she forgot that she had an audience. When she came to the end of the composition, she felt a jolt of surprise as the room erupted in applause. She saw Miss Howe's smiling face, and she saw her Milwaukee family, all beaming and clapping from the front row.

"Oh, that was enthralling!" Millie whispered, after Caroline had returned to her seat. "And you read it so well!"

"Thank you," Caroline murmured. She was still trembling, and her thoughts were jumbled. It took several minutes for her to realize that names were being called. The graduation ceremony had begun. Young ladies were standing and moving forward to accept their diplomas from Miss Mortimer.

After she had received hers, Caroline held the diploma in her hands and gazed down at it.

Milwaukee Female College
Certificate of Graduation
This is to certify that
Caroline Lake Quiner
has graduated with honors
on this 23rd day of May, 1856

Tears welled in Caroline's eyes. She could not wait to show it to Mother.

When the graduation ceremony had come to an end, the families were asked to stay for refreshments, and the scholars were invited to bring Miss Beecher's books they had been given for her to autograph.

Caroline stood in line with Millie waiting her turn. When she finally reached the table, Miss Beecher looked up at her with bright, inquisitive eyes.

"Ah, you are the young lady who read the composition," Miss Beecher said. "A very moving piece, my dear. Have you ever seen the ocean?"

"No ma'am," Caroline replied.

"A good imagination then," Miss Beecher said.

"Thank you," Caroline murmured, and then she quickly said, "I have so enjoyed my time here at the college, Miss Beecher. I have learned a great deal."

"Good—I'm glad to hear it," Miss Beecher replied. "And may I ask what are your plans after you leave here?"

"I wish to be a schoolteacher," Caroline answered. She felt very grown up as she said the words out loud.

Miss Beecher's whole face lit up. "Wonderful! Do you already have a teaching post?"

"No, but I hope to find one close to my home," Caroline said.

"And where is your home?" Miss Beecher asked.

"My family lives near Concord," Caroline replied.

"Ah, I hear much of the interior of Wisconsin is still quite wild," Miss Beecher said.

"Well, it is not so sophisticated as this city," Caroline admitted.

Miss Beecher looked wistful for a moment. "Teachers are always needed on the frontier of our great land, my dear. I wish you well, young lady!" Then she reached out for the book and quickly signed it.

After she had moved away from the table,

Caroline glanced down to see what Miss Beecher had written.

All best wishes in your future endeavors.
Sincerely yours, Catharine Beecher.

The rest of the day was a blur of good-byes. Caroline was glad to leave finally, and get out into the fresh air. Uncle Elisha brought the buggy around and they all climbed in.

The sun was shining brightly overhead as the buggy rolled between the buildings. Caroline gazed at the shop windows and the people rushing to and fro. She thought of how the crowds and noise had scared her at first, but slowly she had grown accustomed to it all.

Uncle Elisha turned toward the lake, and a breeze picked up, so Caroline had to put a hand to her bonnet to keep it straight. The birds dipped and glided overhead in the blue sky, and boys were flying their colorful kites on a bluff overlooking the rocky beach. Sunlight danced across the water.

"What will you do next, Caroline?" Uncle

Elisha asked, breaking the peaceful quiet.

Caroline thought of the last nine months in Milwaukee, and at school. She thought of the people she had met, but most of all, she thought of her family at home. Caroline remembered something her uncle had said when she had first arrived. "No one can predict the future," she said.

Uncle Elisha smiled. "That is the truth, Caroline. That is the truth."

"But for now," Caroline added, "I will go home."